THAT'S A WRAP

PARANORMAL TALENT AGENCY

EPISODE THREE

HEATHER SILVIO

Panther Books

Published in the United States by Panther Books, Las Vegas.

Correspondence to the author may be sent to:
heather@heathersilvio.com

Cover design by Sonia Freitas at Chloe Belle Arts
https://www.ChloeBelleArts.com

ISBN (Print) 978-1-7326938-1-4
ISBN (E-book) 978-1-7326938-4-5

BOOKS BY HEATHER SILVIO

PARANORMAL TALENT AGENCY

Lights, Camera, Action (Episode One)

Reset to One (Episode Two)

That's a Wrap (Episode Three)

An Unexpected Sequel (Episode Four)

Jumping the Shark (Episode Five)

The Season Finale (Episode Six)

NON-SERIES FICTION

Not Quite Famous: A Romantic Comedy of an Actress on the Edge

Beyond the Abyss: Tales of the Supernatural

Courting Death

NONFICTION

Special Snowflake Syndrome: The Unrecognized Personality Disorder Destroying the World

Happiness by the Numbers: 9 Steps to Authentic Happiness

Stress Disorders: A Healing Path for PTSD

ACKNOWLEDGMENTS

Thank you to everyone who supported this series from its original inception to completion. Special thank you to my brand new beta readers!

CHAPTER ONE

One thing I adored after 200 years on the planet was the ever-evolving technology. It still seemed almost like magic to sit in my home office watching someone online, and I happened to know that magic was real. Right now, the lead actor in my movie was starting a Facebook Live video.

"Hi, everybody, I'm Chad Anthony – though hopefully most of you already know that." He laughed, his boyish good looks meshing well with his charming demeanor. He ran his hand through his wavy black hair, the only indication to me that he might be nervous.

We wrapped filming of my latest movie last week and this was the first bit of post-production online marketing. Chad was great. Cute young man. I suspected this would be his breakout role – and I'd been around a long time!

While I'd been admiring his good looks (occupational hazard as a movie producer), he'd continued to talk to his online audience. The likes and the comments floating by on the screen thrilled me.

Chad frowned, and that drew my attention.

"I swear I just heard something." He turned in his chair to check behind him, then back to the laptop camera with a shrug. "Must be the wind knocking a tree branch into a window," he said with a half-smile.

But, now I was frowning. Yes, the weather could differ drastically across the Valley; however the air in my part of Vegas remained dead calm. Could it really be that windy near him? I leaned closer to the screen where Chad had continued to discuss the recently concluded film.

He stopped, his brown eyes narrowing as he turned again to look behind him. "I swear I heard someone. What the heck?"

A mix of comments appeared below the video. People worried for his safety, making fun of Chad for being so jumpy, or flat out accusing him of making this up to increase likes and the likelihood of going viral. Suddenly, loud popping noises came from my laptop. They didn't sound like gunshots, so I quickly dismissed the comments on the video warning Chad that he was about to get shot. Though they did sound familiar. Almost like firecrackers. I couldn't quite put my finger on what the sound reminded me of.

Chad faced the screen, his olive skin paling. "Do you guys hear that? What is it?"

The comments came fast and furious now.

"Get out of the house now!!! This is how someone in LA died!!!"

Wait? What? I tried to grab the user name of the person who typed the comment, but it was already gone, scrolled up and away.

The firecracker noises were louder now and more people were commenting that Chad should call the police, that it couldn't be normal. The young man, on the other hand, seemed frozen in his chair, wide eyes staring at the computer screen. I didn't know if he was reading any of the scrolling comments. I wondered if he saw the one about Los Angeles.

I perched on the edge of my seat, cellphone ready, preparing to call Chad, when the noise abruptly ceased. In the silence, Chad's face relaxed for a mere second before his eyes bugged out and an unseen force pulled him backward from the chair.

My jaw fell open. I stared at the room now visible behind where Chad had been sitting. The comments below the video became frantic. I pressed his number on my phone. I didn't hear it ringing on his end (he listened to me and turned the ringer off, I guessed). When his voicemail engaged, I closed my eyes and took a deep breath. This couldn't be good.

"Hi, you have reached Chad Johnson. If you are interested in auditioning or hiring me for a gig, please call my agent, Catherine Rodham, at Peterson Talent Agency, 702-555-6735. If you need to reach me, you know what to do after the beep."

I stayed silent for a moment, speechless in the face of what I felt fairly confident was going to turn out to be a very bad thing. "Chad, are you okay? It's Mia Fynn, your producer, in case you don't recognize my voice. Or missed my name on the caller ID," I added with a mirthless laugh, babbling. "What did I just see? Call me when you get this. I'm calling the police and will meet them at your place."

While leaving the message, I realized I should have called the police first. I did so now.

"9-1-1, what's your emergency?"

I gave the CliffsNotes version to the dispatcher of what I had seen and she logged the information into her system. I heard a sharp intake of breath before she unexpectedly stated I was the fifth call in the past few minutes to report concern for the young man.

"Did anyone give you his address?"

The dispatcher said yes but asked me for it anyway. I provided the address and told her I'd meet the police officers at the location. She started to tell me that was not a good idea. I thanked her for the commentary and pressed End on my cell.

CHAPTER TWO

Ten minutes later, I pulled up to Chad's apartment complex off West Spring Mountain Road and parked my ruby red Mazda Miata behind a black and white SUV, lights still strobing. I counted at least a half-dozen vehicles as I approached a uniformed officer on the path to Chad's apartment.

"Sorry, no one is allowed through," the officer intoned when I tried to step past him on the concrete walkway.

I peered around him, eager to catch a glimpse of someone I might know. I'd lived in Vegas a long time, maybe I'd get lucky. There!

"Catherine!" I called out to the willowy blond standing next to an attractive man in jeans. She glanced in my direction, half-heartedly waved, and I could tell by her expression I was right to expect a bad outcome.

The officer blocking my way frowned slightly. "Please stay where you are."

Catherine appeared engaged in a deep conversation with the man in jeans, so I realized I would have to handle this on my own. I hated doing it, but desperate times, and all that.

I put on my widest smile. "Officer, I really need to get to my friend." I watched as his frown faltered and his eyes took on the expected glaze.

"I have my orders," he said in a monotone, and I nodded sympathetically.

"Of course, you do. But, it's okay. Isn't it." This last I stated rather than asked.

Slack-jawed, the officer stepped to the side, allowing me passage. I hurried along before the enchantment broke, and joined Catherine and the man, who I realized was law enforcement, judging from the shiny detective's badge clipped to his jeans. My eyes wandered lower and I snapped my gaze up. Good grief.

Catherine enveloped me in a hug, easy since she was several inches taller than me, even without her heels. "He's dead, Mia. He's dead." Her voice cracked and I tightened my embrace.

I felt eyes on me as I released Catherine.

"And who might you be?"

I turned to the voice and watched, bemused, as the detective looked back and forth between me and the officer who abandoned his orders by letting me through. The detective's eyebrow lifted slightly.

"Don't be mad at the officer. I simply explained that I needed to get through," I answered the unasked question.

"Why did you need to get through? Who are you?" he repeated as he took in my appearance.

Inwardly I sighed. Although I was about 200 years old (after a while, who really cared to keep track?) my appearance suggested early-thirties, probably about the same as the detective. I didn't have your typical appearance; my high cheekbones could cut glass and my electric green eyes have been known to stop conversations.

Plus, there was my hair. I watched his eyes move over the emerald green waves that flowed to my waist. I checked him out as well before answering his questions. He looked like a world-weary Captain America, frankly. Blue eyes. Close cut blond hair. A cute crooked nose, probably from being broken at least once. Nice body, maybe a surfer, now or in the past. And, as we silently assessed each other, I felt an itch to touch his lips, his arms, his—what??

"I'm Mia Fynn," I answered with a glance at Catherine, to break the contact with the detective.

"You knew the victim," he responded, his eyes softening when he saw mine pool with unshed tears.

"I produced the movie he was promoting."

"This is Detective Jacob Dawson," Catherine introduced the surfer cop. "He's been assigned to investigate Chad's death."

I closed my eyes and took a deep breath. "What happened?"

"That's what I'm going to find out, Ms. Fynn."

"Please, call me Mia," I said, extending my hand. He automatically reached to grip mine in response, though his attention was elsewhere. Until our skin touched. I pulled my hand abruptly from his as our eyes met.

"Static electricity," I offered with a bark of laughter.

"Uh huh," he responded, his pupils dilating.

Catherine seemed unaware of the sexual tension between me and Jacob. I seized the opportunity to address her. "I take it you saw the Facebook Live."

She nodded. "I was describing it to Jacob when you walked up."

"You saw it too, Ms—Mia."

Tears threatened again. Catherine and I walked the detective through exactly what we both watched. Jacob frowned when we got to the part about Chad being pulled backward by an unseen force.

"An invisible killer?"

"We didn't see anybody," I answered and Catherine agreed. "What did you find in his apartment?" I gestured toward the two-story stucco building behind us.

Jacob stared at me for a long minute. "Why not? It'll be all over the news by tonight, I'm sure." He paused again, gathering his thoughts. "We found the victim – Chad – deceased upon our arrival. We had to break into the apartment."

"Everything was locked? No forced entry?"

Again, Jacob stared at me for a moment. This time Catherine didn't miss the tension, but it was not sexual, it was distrust.

"Mia and I really like those forensics shows," she inserted with a forced laugh.

"No. No forced entry. There was one door in and out. Locked. Windows were closed and locked. From the inside."

I heard the frustration in his voice. I placed a hand on his arm and he startled from the snap of electricity. "Sorry," I said and crossed my arms over my chest.

"Nothing appeared disturbed in the apartment. His computer had gone into sleep mode, but when our tech guy woke it up, or whatever, it was still on Facebook."

"How did he die?" I didn't really want to know, but…

"Suffocation."

"Oh. So not accidental or medical." Having seen the event, I doubted it would be either of those, but I had hoped against hope.

"No."

"None of his neighbors saw or heard anything?" I persisted in asking.

"No." Jacob's eyes narrowed at me.

Catherine's gaze flicked between us again, probably trying to identify why Jacob was suddenly treating me like a suspect. I kind of wanted to know that too. Or maybe he just didn't want civilians acting like armchair detectives. I supposed it didn't really matter. As long as the killer was found.

"I'll let you get back to it, then," I spoke into the silence. As I turned, Jacob touched my shoulder.

"What's your phone number?"

My eyes widened, and he finally smiled.

"In case I have any additional questions," he clarified and a blush burned across my alabaster skin. His smile broadened, and I broke eye contact.

"Of course." I spelled my name for him and provided the requested number. I risked eye contact again before leaving and there was something unreadable in his eyes. He removed a card from his wallet, scribbled on it, and handed it to me.

"My cell is on there too. Text me if you have any additional information." Catherine tilted her head inquisitively at this statement but said nothing. Maybe Jacob didn't usually give out his cellphone number?

"It was nice meeting you," I stated by rote. "I wish it had been under better circumstances."

"It was nice meeting you too," he replied.

I hugged Catherine goodbye, we promised to talk soon, and I walked away. I felt Jacob's eyes on me until I passed into the darkness beyond the streetlights and reached my car. Once inside, a whoosh of air escaped. What on earth was happening to me? It must be the emotions of the evening, I decided, and headed home to replenish my energy.

CHAPTER THREE

Ten minutes later, I was through the gated entrance to my subdivision in The Lakes and pulling into my garage. When people thought of Las Vegas, naturally they thought of the desert, but I needed to live near water and so I did. It was a manmade series of lakes smack in the middle of the Valley. My oasis in the desert. Kinda looked like California, but more affordable.

I breathed deep once I'd entered my home and locked the door behind me. I was more drained than I thought. I fought dizziness and fatigue, stripped off my jeans and tank top, and crossed to the sliding glass doors that opened onto my backyard. I paused beside my pool, debating whether to dive in here, or slip into the lake. Some people made fun of its unnatural colors, but although manmade, it was an actual lake. With fish, turtles, and ducks even.

I walked down the stone stairs to my wooden dock, and slid into the cool water. I dropped below the surface and allowed the water to swaddle me. I could breathe underwater, so I sunk to the bottom.

Fish approached me and I reached out my hands, fingers touching their scaly sides. They knew I belonged, despite looking like the humans they saw through the top of the water. I closed my eyes, my energy store rising.

Air bubbles seeped out of my lungs as I laughed at two fish darting at each other, almost like they were playing a game for my benefit. Showing off. I added my own hand to the play, moving it between them, and soon I'd been accepted as part of it. They moved up to and around my hand, sometimes riding the waves my hand created when I fluttered my fingers. I needed this.

Oh, and I was not a mermaid, though sometimes mythology recorded my kind as such. I was a nixie or naiad, otherwise known as a water spirit. And, although I was long-lived, I was not immortal. Unfortunately. Because how cool would that be?

Once replenished, I floated to the surface. I peered through the prism at the top of the water, making sure nobody was watching. My neighbors have caught me skinny dipping in my pool, but I'd rather not draw attention coming out of the lake. One, we weren't allowed to swim in the water. And, two, it probably looked weird that I'd been underwater for over thirty minutes.

The houses on either side of mine remained dark. I stood motionless on my dock, the water evaporating off me. I resumed moving and my skin was dry by the time I reached the sliding glass door. I entered, staring with longing back where I came. How the water called to me. It might seem strange that a water spirit would live in a desert, but Vegas had its upside. Namely the Paranormal Talent Agency. I chuckled at the nickname for Catherine's office and headed upstairs to take a shower; my lake was not a natural body of water, I wasn't taking the risk of picking up any bacteria!

Later, back at my computer, I decided to look into the Los Angeles murder that Facebook user mentioned. I found one local article, and the few details provided were similar enough to what happened to Chad that my skin crawled. I made a few notes and noticing that it was now after midnight, decided to follow up on it in the morning.

Nightmares plagued my sleep. I watched Chad die over and over again. And even though I didn't see it, my mind created the image of Chad suffocating. I watched him struggle to find breath he never would, petechial hemorrhaging around his eyes, lips turning blue. The light left his eyes as his body, starved of oxygen, lost to the unseen force. The firecracker noise surrounded me in these dreams, taunting me with its familiarity.

The next morning, I woke completely unrested shortly after dawn. Ugh. I was an 8-or-9-hours-of-sleep per night being; getting under six would make for a miserable day. Then I reminded myself that a young man lost his life, sobering my thoughts. Time to see what I could learn. I briefly considered reaching out to Jacob, but after the way he looked at me like a suspect, I decided to try finding something to bring him. Like I was an armchair detective. Exactly what I imagined he would not appreciate, I admitted to myself.

I shrugged and turned on the television to the local news. There was a brief mention of Chad's murder, but nothing new in it. I answered business emails while I had coffee and banana bread; the death of the film's star would impact the release of my movie and there would be other fallout. Time to see what was going to happen.

A couple of hours later, I heard the start of my favorite local morning show, *Entertainment Daily*. Elizabeth Addison, the normally perky brunette co-host, sounded grim as she announced the show's top story. Usually they go for upbeat and, of course, I watched it because I was in the entertainment biz.

I craned my head around my computer to see the screen.

"Last night, a rising actor, on the cusp of stardom, was brutally murdered in his apartment," she began, voice breathy yet sincere. She recapped what I already knew, but then said, "This is the second death under these circumstances. Two weeks ago, an actor in Los Angeles was found dead in his apartment, also following a social media live video. Police there are as stumped as our local Metro PD. Could these two be connected?"

The image cut to Jacob Dawson, glaring into the camera as he growled "No comment" at Elizabeth.

"That video was taken last night outside Chad's apartment complex. Police are being tight-lipped about any information they may or may not have thus far in both of these cases. We'll keep you updated."

I sat back in my wicker chair. Damn. Elizabeth was going hard-core. She seemed pretty interested in these cases. I wondered what else she might know that she wasn't revealing.

*****

An hour later, I stood in the lobby of the station waiting for the receptionist on the other side of the glass to let Elizabeth Addison know that Mia Fynn would like to see her. "Please tell her I'm the producer on the movie Chad Johnson shot right before his untimely death." I could tell the newscaster was hungry for information on that story. If anything would get her to see me, I was certain that was it.

Sure enough, the receptionist smiled at me and said, "Ms. Addison will be out shortly."

"Thank you," I responded and sat on the uncomfortable blue plastic chairs in the lobby, leaning my laptop bag against my leg. I glanced around at the headshots of the on-air talent while I waited. Not five minutes later, toothy smile wide, short curly brown hair perfectly coifed, Elizabeth Addison opened the locked door and strode toward me, hand outstretched. If she was taken aback by my green hair, she masked it.

"I'm Liz Addison," she said without preamble. "You must be Mia Fynn?"

I nodded and shook her hand. Strong grip.

"Let's head back to my office."

I nodded again and followed her back through the door, hearing it automatically lock behind us. We walked down a narrow hallway, into and through a wide cubicle-filled noisy main floor, and back to a corner office. Floor-to-ceiling windows separated the office from the cubicle area. I was impressed by the soundproofing when utter silence remained after she closed her door.

Liz indicated a chair opposite her utilitarian desk. "Please, have a seat." She waited a nanosecond after my butt hit the chair before talking. "So, you're the producer of Chad Johnson's movie?" I nodded and she continued. "What can I do for you?" There was an odd glint to her eyes, flashed so briefly I wondered if I imagined it, and then she was back to her folksy open newscaster persona. I tilted my head for a moment, considering, before letting it go and focusing on my reason for approaching her.

"I caught your story this morning on Chad," I started, my voice catching on his name. I cleared my throat. "I also am aware of the LA murder and was curious what else you knew, that maybe you held back in the broadcast."

Liz frowned. "No, unfortunately, I don't know any more information," she acknowledged. "I was hoping you might, and that's why you wanted to see me."

I heard the disappointment in her voice. "Right," I responded, mainly as a delay tactic, while I thought about where to go with my questioning.

Liz's brown eyes sparkled. "Although…"

I resisted the temptation to roll my eyes at her theatrics. "Yes…," I played along.

"I do have a source in LA," she said with a small coy smile.

"That's awesome," I reacted with more enthusiasm than warranted, because I sensed that was what she wanted.

"But…"

Oh, good grief. This woman would drive me batty if she kept this up. "Liz, do you or do you not have access to additional information?" I asked this sternly and it had the desired effect.

Liz dropped the act. "Yeah, I do. She's a detective in LA. She says she'll give me copies of what she has on the first murder."

"That's great. There must be something that will help us figure out what happened to Chad."

"It's not that easy," she warned. "She'll only give it to me in person."

"Hmm," I muttered. "Go to LA?"

"Yep."

It was a likely four-hour drive there and back, and that was *if* traffic cooperated getting in and out of Vegas. Not to mention the nightmare that was LA traffic. Or we could fly, but then we'd have the hassle at the airport, plus needing to rent a car. My brain screamed at me about needing more sleep, but if it could help solve Chad's murder, it'd be worth it.

"Oh, and I need to be back in time for tomorrow morning's broadcast," Liz added with a wicked smile.

I couldn't help it but I laughed. "You're enjoying this, aren't you?"

She sobered briefly. "I wish it was under different circumstances. But, yeah. This is what I went into journalism to do."

"You didn't do it to cover the latest It Girl's movie?"

Liz rolled her eyes then shrugged. "Nah, but that's kind of fun too," she admitted.

I calculated in my head. "We have about sixteen hours to drive to LA, meet with your source, possibly do any follow up, and drive back."

"Sounds about right." She smiled the first genuine smile I'd seen that morning. "What do you say?"

"Road trip." I mirrored her smile.

CHAPTER FOUR

Liz and I left straight from the studio, although I insisted on a quick stop first. "I need an energy boost," I explained.

Since Liz knew I was up late last night at the crime scene, she understood. She maneuvered her white Audi R8 Coupe (clearly being a media personality in Vegas paid better than I thought!) out of the station's parking lot and eased into traffic. We headed for the 215, watching for a Starbucks. Liz shot across three lanes of traffic when she spotted one and pulled into the drive thru. Thankfully, there were only two cars in front of us. It was amazing how often the line stretched into the street.

"What do you want?" Liz asked this as we pulled forward to order.

"Espresso macchiato, with an extra shot of espresso."

I heard the smile in her voice when she placed my order, getting a small house brew for herself. "I don't do fancy drinks," she tossed over her shoulder at me.

I laughed. "Your loss." In a few minutes, I sipped at my beverage of the gods. Appropriately caffeinated, we hit the road.

We drove the 215 to the 15 and followed the signs to Los Angeles. We were both pleasantly surprised that the traffic was light. Soon we left Sin City behind, heading toward the City of Angels. There was a joke in there somewhere, but I was still too tired to find it.

Our ride was uneventful as we passed through Primm, Barstow, and Victorville on our four-hour drive. Well, four-and-a-half hours. We did have to make a bathroom stop. Signs for San Bernardino informed us we were close, so Liz sent a quick text message to her contact, requesting an exact site for meeting.

"That seems a bit cloak-and-dagger," I commented. "Not to give us the meeting location ahead of time."

"She's a cop. They're paranoid by nature. Plus, she's violating her department's rules," she reminded me with a side glance.

I lifted my hands in a mea culpa. "That's true."

Liz watched for the exit off the 210 for Highland Park, our apparent meeting place. We exited Figueroa and within another ten minutes found ourselves near the neighborhood.

"Where are we meeting your contact?"

Liz laughed as she turned onto York. "Starbucks."

Hmm. Maybe I'd have a second coffee. I pointed to the building across from a 99cent store.

Easing the car into a space, we exited and stretched after the long drive. Liz opened the door to the squat building and a wiry Latina seated just inside lifted her chin at Liz in greeting. I followed her over to the table and we sat across from the officer.

"I'm Selina," she introduced herself, and I didn't miss that she only offered her first name.

"Mia."

"Do you have the files?" Liz drummed her fingers on the table in anticipation.

Selina placed her hand flat on the table and slid it toward us. When she removed her hand, a small thumb drive remained there. Liz quickly disappeared it into her pocket. "Be careful."

"Of course," Liz replied dismissively.

Selina's eyes darkened. "Seriously. Roger Miller was suffocated in a manner we can't identify. If what you're saying in Vegas is true, his killer has struck again."

"Thank you for the warning," I said, cutting my eyes at Liz. She really could be more appreciative and less cavalier. "And I know it's probably in the files. But, any suspects?" Selina shook her head. "Anything that stood out as unusual?"

"Other than the locked room?" she asked sarcastically.

"Yeah, other than that."

"There was one thing," she began, her eyes clouding over. "It didn't seem connected."

Liz and I waited for her to continue.

"Mr. Miller had a generally clean record with one notable exception."

My goodness, this was like pulling teeth.

Liz was a good deal less patient. "C'mon Selina, spit it out. We've got to get back to Vegas." They stared at each other for a beat and I wondered what their relationship really was. And then Selina dropped the bombshell.

"A year prior to his death, Roger Miller was investigated for the disappearance and possible murder of his girlfriend."

I sat back in the plastic chair in shock. Maybe Roger was a killer and his murder was revenge? "Wait, you said it didn't seem connected," I challenged.

"Yep. We investigated that angle and nothing really seemed to come of it." Selina unexpectedly chuckled at the matching expectant looks on our faces.

"Okay, okay. I'll tell you what we learned. 9-1-1 received a call from a motorist who had pulled off to the side of the road. The couple saw a damaged guardrail and the wife thought she saw light reflecting off of something metallic over the side in the bushes. The husband went down the side and found the wrecked car. Roger Miller was alone in the vehicle, unconscious and bleeding from several scrapes, but nothing that looked severe.

"We later learned at the hospital it was a combination of alcohol and head trauma that knocked him out. The passenger door was closed. There was no evidence that anybody else was or had been recently in the vehicle. Miller did not respond to the husband's attempts to rouse him, though it was confirmed he was breathing.

"The husband noted a piece of the guardrail had flipped up and pierced the windshield into the front passenger seat. First responders arrived and transported Miller to the hospital. When he awoke, he kept asking for his girlfriend, Juni. He insisted she was in the car with him. If," she stressed the word, "someone had been in that seat, he or she would have been impaled and would not have walked away from the accident."

My eyes widened slightly before I recovered. Vampire? That could explain a passenger who was there and then not there following an impaling. I made a mental note to check with my one and only vampire friend, Evie, when we returned to Vegas. She was an actress I met through the Paranormal Talent Agency, of course. I focused on Selina's voice.

"Here's where it gets weird."

"You mean it wasn't weird yet?" Liz asked with a chuckle and Selina smiled.

"Weirder," she amended. "Here's where it gets weirder. The easiest way to show that the girlfriend, Juni, wasn't in the car would be to find her, happy and whole. Right?"

We nodded and she continued.

"This kid, Miller, didn't have a last name for her, said he'd only known her a couple of months, and only had a partial picture. She had no other friends he knew of, nor where she worked, or even where she lived. We blasted what little we had over the local news and social media. We asked the public if they knew who this woman was. Nothing. No missing report was ever filed in LA that matched her picture. We entered her information into the national database and never got legitimate hits. It's like this girl popped into existence and then popped right back out." Frustration tinged every word of her statement.

Definitely vampire. The more Selina spoke, the more convinced I was.

"We charged Roger Miller with driving while intoxicated and reckless driving for his likely speed and no evidence of braking before the crash. But," she shrugged, "without a body, or any evidence this young lady even existed, there wasn't much else to do. He got court-ordered drug therapy and six-months' probation."

Liz and I sat quietly for a moment, processing all the information.

Selina looked at her watch. "If you don't have any other questions…" She waited half a second for Liz and me to shake our heads no and then she stood. "I've got to get back to work. I hope it helps," she said sincerely. "Don't be shy in sharing any of your information either."

We agreed to do so and remained seated as Selina left.

"What do you think?" I finally asked Liz.

"I think we need to review those files and then look into Roger Miller before we leave Los Angeles."

Her excitement was infectious and I smiled. "I was hoping you'd say that!"

After grabbing more coffees, we spent the next fifteen minutes staring at my laptop screen. Selina was nothing if not thorough. She provided us with copies of Roger Miller's autopsy report, the Facebook Live video of his murder, and scores of interviews with folks identified as his friends, family, or people of interest (although unfortunately, as Selina had stated, not as potential suspects). We reviewed the paperwork before watching the video. When we saw the side profile picture of Juni, we paused to take in the twenty-something raven-haired beauty. Oh, and vampires could have their picture taken, so this neither confirmed nor eliminated my hunch that she was a vampire.

"Witness protection program," I joked.

"Right? Who doesn't have a single social media account or even just a basic online footprint in this day and age?" Liz agreed.

"It is odd."

I brought up the Facebook Live video and made sure my sound was way down – didn't want to frighten anybody around us. The video was almost eerily identical to Chad's and I felt a lump in my throat at the fear both of these men had before being violently killed. We had to find something that would help solve these murders and prevent others.

Liz and I sat in silence for a few moments following the conclusion of the video. "Next step?" Liz asked.

"Let's talk to Roger Miller's mother before we head back to Vegas. Maybe her son told her something more or different than what he told the police following Juni's disappearance."

CHAPTER FIVE

Thirty minutes later we pulled behind a blue Honda Accord in the driveway of a modest Spanish Colonial home. I noted the well-kept lawn and bright flowers as we walked up the concrete path to the red front door. We did not call ahead, so I was hoping the car meant his mother was home. I glanced at my watch and cringed when I saw it was already 8 p.m. Liz knocked as I glanced up and down the street. Minimal traffic, no pedestrians. Definitely a suburban area. The door opened to reveal a middle-aged woman with bloodshot eyes holding a tissue.

"May I help you?"

Part of me wanted to back away from this clearly grieving woman – what were we thinking? – but Liz had already extended her hand. "Mrs. Miller?"

"Yes?"

"Roger Miller's mother?"

Her eyes clouded over and a single tear tracked down her cheek. She appeared resigned. "Are you with the press?"

I jumped in before Liz could answer in the affirmative. "Ma'am, we are so sorry for your loss. We heard about Roger's murder…" Mrs. Miller visibly paled at the word. "…while investigating the murder of my friend, Chad Johnson. You may have seen something about it on the news?"

Mrs. Miller thought for a moment. "I haven't seen or heard anything. But, then I've barely gotten out of bed," she directed this towards me, almost defiantly.

"I don't blame you," I simply said and the dam broke. Mrs. Miller audibly cried as she indicated we should follow her into the home.

Dark with all the blinds drawn and few lights turned on, I could tell even in the gloom that hers was a cared for home. My heart broke for the loss this mother had experienced.

"Please sit down," she directed us to a sectional couch in a pale blue abstract design. Liz and I sat on the edge of the sofa while Mrs. Miller moved to the loveseat facing us. Her hands lay limply in her lap.

"Mrs. Miller," I started, and she stopped me.

"Please call me Jacki," she said by rote.

I hesitated. Liz wisely remained quiet, to see how this played out. "Jacki, my friend and I are trying to gather information related to your son's death that might help us understand what happened to our friend, Chad, and prevent anyone else from being hurt. But, if this is too painful, we can leave."

Jacki raised her face and looked at us through watery eyes. "It's okay. Not talking about it won't bring him back. If I can help some other mother not go through this, then I will." She took a long, shuddering breath. "Ask your questions."

I brought Jacki through our understanding of the events that transpired on the night of the car accident and she confirmed that Roger told her the same story he provided the police, and that she had no reason to doubt what he said.

"Even though he'd been drinking?" I asked gently and Jacki looked away briefly before responding.

"Roger had only recently turned 21. He was still sowing his wild oats when it came to alcohol. He had made a couple of bad choices, but never anything like that. He'd never blacked out or hurt anyone."

Not that you know of, I thought to myself before refocusing on Jacki.

"I had no reason to doubt that he genuinely believed Juni had been in the car with him," she concluded.

"How do you explain the lack of evidence of anybody in the passenger seat?" Liz asked this.

"I don't."

That stumped us and for a moment nobody said anything. "We spoke to the police about Juni," I restarted the conversation. "It seems nobody really knew her well."

"I only met her once," Jacki stated. "Juni and Roger had only been dating a couple of months, but he was smitten with her." A genuine smile ghosted across her face then faded. "She never gave my son her last name."

"You didn't think that was odd?" Liz asked, doubt tinging her voice.

"At first, but Roger explained Juni said she had escaped an abusive relationship. She told him she didn't want to endanger him."

"Is that why there's only the one picture of her?" This made more sense to me now; although, not if she was a vampire. Hmm. Jacki was still explaining.

"She was worried about being found, so she didn't want any pictures. I snapped that one. She was very unhappy with me and asked me to delete the picture. I lied and told her I did." Jacki's face reddened at the remembrance of the deception. "I just wanted one picture," she finished defensively.

"I think it's okay," I assured her and she smiled gratefully before her mouth turned downward.

"After the accident, Roger spent weeks searching the area near the crash, first with the actual search parties and then on his own. He confided to me that he was having nightmares of her alone and scared in the woods."

My heart broke again for that grieving young man, trying to process the strange loss of his love.

"Once he finished his probation, he finally seemed ready to rejoin the world. I was so happy to have my son back," she said wistfully. "Then to have him taken again, forever." Her voice choked on the last word and she stared at her wringing fingers in her lap.

Liz and I shared a glance. We'd likely gotten all that we could from Roger's mom. I stood and Liz followed my cue. "Jacki, thank you so much for taking the time to speak with us."

She scrambled to her feet. "Was anything I said helpful?"

I smiled gently. "Yes. You've given us a few new angles to consider."

"I'm glad," she said. "You'll tell me if you find who did this to our boys?"

"Of course." I nodded and she clasped my hands in hers. On impulse I hugged her. She tensed but then relaxed.

"Thank you for listening."

Jacki watched us walk back to our car and we considered our next steps while we drove from her home.

"What do you think?" Sadness hung on me from Jacki and I needed to focus on something active.

"Let's head back to Vegas," Liz declared. "We can review what we have."

I concurred, though of course, directed Liz to the nearest coffee dispensing establishment, a Dunkin Donuts this time.

"Let's do some internet sleuthing and then review the information Selina provided," I suggested once we were back on the road for our four-and-a-half-hour drive home. Liz agreed and explained the Audi's awesome wifi hotspot capability.

I googled "Juni Los Angeles" and frowned at the screen.

"What?" Liz glanced over at me.

"Nothing, that's what. Absolutely nothing of use. The big goose egg. Nada." I was trying to think of another expression for nothing when Liz laughed.

"No more caffeine for you."

"Am I a little hyper?"

"Yeah, I'd say so." Liz paused. "It really is weird how there's nothing on Juni No-Last-Name. Even if she decided to drop off the grid, you can't erase your past like that. Unless she really was in the witness protection program."

Or she was a vampire, I silently added.

"What is it? You've got this weird expression on your face. I noticed it last time we talked about her having no history." Liz narrowed her eyes at me. "Spill it."

CHAPTER SIX

I widened my eyes in a parody of innocence. "I have no idea what you're talking about." I broke eye contact. I was not about to tell Liz I thought Juni was a vampire.

"Fine. Keep your little secret," Liz said, her tone light, but with an undercurrent of something darker.

"I agree it's weird that she truly seems to have popped in and out of existence," I repeated what Selina had said earlier. "An alternative explanation is that her first name is fake too."

"Hmm. That would make sense. And with no good pictures to run a google image search on, that would be an effective way for her to mask her history," Liz agreed. "Where does that leave us then?"

"Let's take a look at Roger Miller's social media accounts," I suggested and was already typing away on the laptop. A quick scroll through his Facebook, Twitter, and Instagram accounts confirmed the mother's reports. "He really was in love – and really depressed and guilty after the accident."

"Guess he shouldn't have been driving drunk," Liz snapped.

"Harsh, Liz. He was a dumb kid who made a mistake. You never made a mistake before?"

Liz lifted a single shoulder dismissively. "This isn't about me."

"That's true," I responded and closed the open browser tab. "Let's review what Selina gave us," I changed the subject.

The miles passed by in a blur (except for a single bathroom break, of course) as we reviewed each of the files. While watching Roger's Facebook Live video again, I had that same sense of déjà vu hearing the firecracker noise and made a slight grunt of irritation.

"What?"

"I don't know. There's something about that popping noise that I can't place and I know that I should be able to." Frustration was audible in my voice.

"You had the same reaction with Chad's video?"

"I did." I scrunched up my face trying to place the noise. I sighed loudly and slumped in the seat. "This is ridiculous."

Liz laughed. "Don't be so hard on yourself. Quit thinking about it and maybe it'll come to you."

"What do you think about Selina's conclusion that Juni's disappearance and the murder aren't related?"

"It could be a coincidence," Liz spoke slowly, thinking. "But. It seems like too big an event NOT to be connected. On the other hand, if it is connected, I'm having a hard time seeing how."

"Maybe Juni faked her death with the plan to come back and kill Roger when the heat had died down," I suggested my outlandish explanation with a giggle.

"Oh, I'm sure that's it," Liz agreed with a laugh. Soon we were both giggling at the ridiculousness of the idea. Clearly, she was right and I'd had too much caffeine!

After that, we sang along to the radio and made idle chitchat, letting our brains percolate with the information we'd gathered. Liz pulled into the television station parking lot and dropped me next to my car.

"I'll check in with you after my show."

"Give me a few more hours to get some sleep," I requested with a lopsided smile. "When I crash from the caffeine, it ain't gonna be pretty."

"Okay, get back to me when you're awake. We'll talk more about our next steps." She glanced at her watch. "I'm off to catch a few winks myself."

"Sounds good," I agreed and Liz drove off. I sat in my car for a moment. It wouldn't be dawn for a few hours, so I took a chance and texted Evie.

You home?

Sure. Isn't this a bit early for you?

I have some questions, best done in person.

Uh-oh. Everything okay?

With me, yes. I need your help with something.

Come on over.

I drove towards the Arts District and Evie's condo. A parking spot opened up directly in front of the building as I passed through the final light and I zipped the Miata into the space. The front desk attendant had apparently been alerted that I was coming. When I showed him my ID, he didn't call Evie to let her know I'd arrived and instead waved me through to the elevators.

The ping of the elevator door sounded loud in the early morning silence when it opened on Evie's floor. I saw her door was slightly propped open; I knocked as quietly as I could.

"I'm coming in, Evie."

"Welcome!" was her response from around the corner in the condo.

I closed the door behind me and had taken only a few steps when both my phone and Evie's dinged with incoming text messages. She was faster than me at checking and laughed. "It's Catherine. She wants to know if she can come over."

I confirmed that was the text I received and responded yes. A slight knock on the door followed almost immediately. I opened it to Catherine's wide smile.

"I heard the elevator and then your voice. I figured it must be something interesting."

"I know why Evie's up, but why are you?"

"I was up early for a production starting today. On-call in case of any problems," Catherine explained, long blond hair pulled up in a ponytail. She closed and locked the door behind her. As the only human in the room, security was more of an issue for her than us.

Soon we were seated on Evie's couch, me marveling as I always did about her fabulous view of the city. The women turned to me.

"What's going on?" Evie asked, blue eyes curious.

I brought them up to speed about the two murders and my trip to LA with Liz Addison. Evie was frowning before I could finish.

"I'm almost 100% certain there was no vampire in Vegas named Juni," she asserted. "Now, if you're right that she was using an entirely faked name, there's less certainty. Although I haven't heard anything about any vampires vanishing either. Of course, we don't check in and out of the city, so it would be possible for her to come and go if she's from here. I have no idea about LA. I can check with my people." She sent a quick text. "Show me her picture."

Evie and Catherine chatted while I turned on the laptop and brought up the half-profile image of our missing, presumed dead, woman, maybe vampire, Juni.

Evie frowned at the picture. "She doesn't look familiar at all." Her phone beeped with an incoming text and she glanced down. "Nobody fitting the description missing in LA, either. Probably not a vampire. Most likely just a drunk guy who is misremembering his evening."

Disappointment surged through me. I didn't know why I wanted Juni to be a vampire so badly. Maybe because then there might be some motive for Roger's murder? Although that wouldn't explain Chad's murder.

"Earth to Mia," Catherine said with a laugh, waving her hand in front of my face. I refocused on my friends.

"Sorry, guys. It just seemed important to me that Juni was a vampire. I really don't know why."

"Do you want to go through the rest of your material? Maybe Catherine and I will see something that you and Liz missed."

I thanked Evie for the offer and we methodically moved through each of the documents. The autopsy report confirmed suffocation, like we expected with Chad's forthcoming report, but no evidence on the body of how. No strangulation marks on the neck, for example.

The interviews of family and friends were the typical, *I can't believe this happened to him*, type of responses. We found it interesting how few people mentioned Juni.

Then we reached the last piece of evidence we had — the Facebook Live video. Between seeing Chad's in real time, and the multiple viewings of Roger's, I no longer wanted to watch. I faced my head away and tilted the screen more toward Catherine and Evie.

"Do you guys hear that popping noise? What is that?" Roger's words, so eerily similar to Chad's, pierced my heart. These poor young men, snuffed out before their lives had really even started.

I bolted upright just as Evie shouted.

"I know what that is!"

She and I faced each other and simultaneously exclaimed, "Djinn!"

Catherine looked back and forth between us, clearly not following. But, we'd figured it out. I sat back down and patted Catherine's knee, smiling at Evie.

"It's been bothering me since I first watched Chad's Facebook Live video. That popping noise, so much like firecrackers, sounded familiar. I just couldn't place it. And each time I watched Roger's, the same. Now I know."

"The murderer is a djinn," Evie added, which increased Catherine's confusion.

"A djinn is better known as a genie," I explained.

"How do you know that noise is from a genie?"

"If a djinn is angry enough, and this one must be to want to kill people, they create a popping noise that is a physical manifestation of that anger," Evie said.

"That means that even though I was wrong about her being a vampire, I was also probably right about Juni," I added. Catherine looked confused again.

"A djinn is an elemental being. When one dies, it reverts back to its element. If Juni was stabbed by the metal of the guardrail through the heart, that would certainly have killed her." I felt a moment of sadness at the death of the immortal, but not invincible, being.

"And since she would have reverted back to her elemental nature, there would be no evidence of her in the car."

The three of us considered the possibilities.

"How do you think that's connected to the murders?" Evie asked.

"I'm not sure," I answered as my mind worked through the logic. "I'm not aware of any djinn in Vegas…" Evie shook her head no, that she wasn't either.

"Since the first murder took place in LA, the djinn could be there. I don't know anyone to ask. We should operate on the assumption that the djinn could be in either city and travelled back and forth," I finished.

"Do you think this djinn will kill anyone else?" Catherine asked in a small voice.

"Since we don't know the motive behind the murders, I think we should assume it's likely," I answered grimly. "Even if the first murder is related to Juni's death, that doesn't explain Chad."

"He has zero connection to the paranormal as far as I know," Catherine added.

We pondered this inconsistency.

"There is a possibility," Evie said as she stood and walked toward the sliding glass doors leading to her balcony. She stopped and stared out into the dark. "I may be misremembering my elemental being knowledge, but aren't many djinn born as twins?"

I gasped. "Oh, my goodness. You might be on to something!" I stood as well and paced back and forth in front of the couch while I worked through this new angle. "If Juni had a twin, that djinn could be our killer. How do we find her? Or him?"

Evie frowned. "I think the twins are usually same-sex, but honestly, I don't really know. I think, either way, we'll have a heck of a time finding a djinn that probably doesn't want to be found."

"Why?" Catherine asked.

"Oh, djinn are fun," Evie answered with a laugh.

I explained further. "They can shape shift, fly, and become invisible."

"Ah, those *would* make it difficult," Catherine agreed and the three of us chuckled. "What do you want to do?"

"I want to talk to Detective Dawson," I blurted out.

Catherine arched an eyebrow. "Jacob?"

Evie looked confused. "Who?

"Detective Jacob Dawson is investigating Chad's murder," Catherine explained to Evie.

"Is he…like us?" Evie asked.

I shook my head no.

"Then why would we want to tell him anything? Would you tell him everything?"

"Of course not, Evie. But," I continued before she could interrupt, "if we give him the background, leaving out that Juni was probably a djinn, we can tell him to look for a sister. With the risk this sister poses to humanity, let alone exposing all of us with her actions, it's imperative we find her sooner rather than later. Maybe with their additional databases and stuff, Jacob'll have better luck."

"I guess that makes sense," Evie reluctantly agreed.

"And the LA cop too, right?" Catherine asked.

"I'll let Liz know and she can tell Selina. We just leave the paranormal stuff out of all of it," I concluded and the other women nodded in agreement.

A narrow band of light was surfacing over the mountain range outside the city. Evie gestured to it. "Sun is coming up, ladies, so I'll need to kick you out now. Time for my beauty sleep."

CHAPTER SEVEN

Sitting in my car, watching the light brighten around me as the sun came up, I considered my options. It was barely daytime. The detective was probably not even awake yet. Although Liz definitely was, she was likely prepping for her show in a couple of hours. The best thing, I decided, as I started my engine, was to go home and get my own beauty sleep for a few hours. I was truly running on fumes, after being up for … how many hours? I started counting backwards to determine how long I'd been awake and then realized this was further proof of my exhaustion. Time to return to The Lakes.

Unfortunately, with the sun up, a skinny dip in the lake was not a good idea. I decided a quick swim in my pool would have to suffice. And I guessed I'd be neighborly and wear a swimsuit. Once inside my home, I padded silently across the natural stone floor while I stripped my clothes off. I grabbed the aquamarine one-piece off the back of the wicker chair in the breakfast nook (its permanent home when I wasn't wearing it) and slid the glass door open. Stepping out onto the concrete, I breathed in the crisp morning air. The mountains were visible in the distance.

Water caressed my skin as I dropped beneath the surface of the pool. No underwater life lived here so I swam a few laps, flipped a few somersaults for fun, and practiced what I liked to call, mermaid maneuvers. I realized I was smiling underwater and settled to the bottom. Colorful pebble-tec instead of boring plaster coated my pool and I delighted in the dolphin, turtle, and seal I had custom designed for the floor.

Despite the replenishing qualities of the water, the exhaustion from lack of actual sleep threatened to overwhelm me. I surfaced with reluctance. I felt someone's eyes on me and a quick glance to my left identified the source.

"Hi, Elliott," I called out to my neighbor and swam to the side closest to our shared wall. He had a dazed look on his face.

"How—?" he asked, and I groaned under my breath. I knew better than to stay underwater so long during the daytime.

I hoisted myself out of the pool and began the short walk to where he stood on the other side of the shared concrete wall. His eyes tracked the water dripping off my slender figure. I squeezed the extra water from my long green hair and flashed a bright smile at my befuddled neighbor.

"You aren't going to sing me to my death, Mia, are you?" He asked with a nervous laugh, probably his idea of flirtation. I managed not to roll my eyes at his not-so-subtle joke that I was a siren. This was why humanity couldn't know about us. They wouldn't even get it right!

"Of course not, Elliott," I responded, modulating my voice slightly and watching his eyes glaze in response. "You didn't see anything out of the ordinary, did you, Elliott?" I'd reached where he stood opposite and touched his arm resting atop the short wall.

"Like what, Mia?" he asked in a daze.

"Exactly, Elliott." I smiled and saw that he was completely mesmerized. My green eyes sparkled and I giggled, the sound of a tinkling bell. "You enjoy the rest of your day, Elliott." He nodded like an excited puppy and I turned before I broke the spell with a real laugh. I felt his eyes watching me walk away, back toward my sliding glass door. After opening it, I turned to give him a slight wave goodbye, and then closed the door tightly.

I really hated entrancing humans when it was my fault they saw something they shouldn't. The need for discretion was always present. I knew better. Sometimes, though, the water just called to me. I shrugged even though nobody was watching, peeled off the wet bathing suit, and returned it to the back of the wicker chair before trudging up the stairs to my bedroom for a well-deserved nap.

Hours later, I woke finally refreshed physically and emotionally. My phone showed a text from Liz letting me know she was free. Before I called, I sent a quick text to Jacob, asking if he had time to meet today and where.

"Hey, Mia," Liz answered the call. Apparently, I'd already made it onto her Contacts list. I smiled.

"Hey, Liz, how was the show?"

"Very good. How was your nap?"

"Excellent." Chit chat out of the way, I dove right in. "I may have some new info. I thought I'd swing by and pick you up, then we could go see Jacob."

"Ooo, what new info?" I could hear the reporter in her salivating at my words.

I laughed. "I'm gonna make you wait."

"Tease."

"Are you at the studio or home?"

"Studio."

"Be there in fifteen." Ending the call, I read the response from Jacob that he was at headquarters for training today and to let him know when we'd arrived.

*****

Liz still wore remnants of her show makeup, I saw, when she opened the passenger door and hopped in my car. She'd changed into a t-shirt and jeans, though, from whatever fancy dress she wore for the show this morning.

"What do you know?"

"A friend of mine who knows people," I started, deliberately vague because I wasn't sharing Evie's paranormal status – and I knew it would drive Liz crazy.

"What friend? Who does she know?" I flashed a smile and Liz shook her head. "Fine. Continue."

"My friend who knows people said that although we don't have a last name for Juni, my friend has reason to believe we should be looking for a sister."

Liz's mouth fell open. "What… where… how… I don't understand," she finally completed a statement. Her mouth twisted while she thought.

"Without a last name at all, and uncertainty whether the first name is even real, how on earth could your friend, no matter what she does or who she knows, possibly have deduced that there's a sister?" Liz stared at me, her look indecipherable.

I made a noncommittal noise. "She just does."

"How are we going to bring this to Selina and Jacob? They're police officers," she needlessly reminded me. "There's no way they're going to accept this information, without thinking we know more than we're sharing with them. Do we know more than we're sharing?" She asked this question, a shrewd look on her face as she tried to figure out where I was coming from.

"That's all I can say," I replied honestly. Even if I trusted Liz more, she was a newscaster. There was zero chance if I told her the paranormal angle that it wouldn't wind up all over her show in the morning. I wasn't dumb.

"Hmm." Liz removed her phone from her purse and sent a text. Less than a minute later, her phone dinged, several times in a row, announcing responses. "Shocker. Selina wants to know how I could know this, who told me, and what more do I know." She gave me the side eye. "What should I tell her?"

I knew her question was mostly rhetorical, but I ticked off the answers to Selina's questions anyway. "You have your sources, you don't disclose your sources, and that's all you're willing to share right now."

"Or, how about this?" she countered. "I have my source, her name is Mia, and she's hiding the rest of the information."

The clear irritation in her voice surprised me. She was a reporter, after all; she should understand protecting sources. I guess she just wasn't used to being denied. "We'll start with this," I said gently. "And see what happens."

She nodded her head, though the crossed arms and frown suggested less agreement. Before she could say anything else, we arrived at Metro headquarters.

CHAPTER EIGHT

I pulled into the parking lot off of MLK Blvd and headed to the building on the left. Once inside, I texted Jacob. Two volunteers in bright yellow shirts sat behind a glass partition with a small opening at the bottom.

"We're here to see Detective Jacob Dawson," I announced to the hole. "He's on his way to get us."

"ID please," came the response.

Liz and I slid our driver's licenses through the hole, the volunteer dutifully made a note of our information.

"Phone number?" We each rattled this off. The door to the left clicked then opened as the volunteer slid visitor badges on lanyards through the hole. "Wear these at all times in the building and return them on your way out."

"Thank you," I spoke into the hole, before turning to Jacob walking through the open door. "Perfect timing, Detective Dawson."

The detective's eyes took in my appearance again – occupational hazard, or should I take this personally? Sheesh. I almost wanted to strike a pose for his benefit, but it wouldn't be that impressive, with my hair in a high ponytail, green t-shirt, and jeans over green wedges. He, on the other hand, looked business casual nice, with a short-sleeved blue shirt over dark khakis and boots.

My eyes finished their exploration and he had a soft smile when I met his gaze. "Good afternoon, Ms. Fynn. And Ms. Addison," he added a beat later, his expression souring when he recognized the newscaster.

"Try not to be so happy to see me," she quipped.

"What can I do for you ladies?"

"Liz and I took a field trip to LA," I started, "to look into the other Facebook Live murder."

Jacob's eyes were unreadable in an impassive face. "Okay."

"We uncovered some information we think may be helpful," I continued with a big smile. See how helpful I could be? He didn't bite.

"How did you investigate that case in another city? Friends in high places?"

"Wouldn't you like to know?" Liz retorted coyly and Jacob stiffened.

"What did you find out?"

I quickly brought him up to speed, skipping over the part with Selina giving us copies of department documents, and instead focusing on the deceased's social media info and our talk with his mother.

"We have an unexpected new direction you can pursue," Liz finished with a sly smile. "We're hoping to make a deal."

"We are?" Liz shot me a look and I realized I said that out loud. Would have been nice if she had clued me in beforehand.

"We'll give you our information if you promise me an exclusive when you learn more."

"I don't have the authority to make a deal like that, Ms. Addison," Jacob said tonelessly.

"You're a detective, aren't you?"

"I'm on a team. It doesn't work like that."

"Yes, it does."

"No, it doesn't. And I'm not going to argue with you like we're children. If you don't wish to share your information without a quid pro quo…," he turned to head back to the locked door.

"Jacob, wait!" He turned back, more at my use of his first name than my request, I would guess. My face reddened. "I'll give you what we have."

"What?!"

"Liz, I get that you want the scoop, but solving the murder is more important," I explained to my indignant partner. She harrumphed and crossed her arms. Jacob was now smiling.

"Look, Ms. Addison, I can try. That's the best I can agree to," he offered.

"I'll accept that," she agreed, mollified at least a little by his concession.

"We believe the murders of Roger Miller in LA and Chad Johnson here were committed by the same person," I began.

Jacob nodded. "LAPD and I agree."

"We also believe that the murders may be related to Roger's girlfriend, Juni."

"We looked at that angle and dismissed it," Jacob disagreed.

"Why?" Liz asked.

Jacob paused before answering. "Juni had no connection to the victim here; and she was long-gone or long-dead by the time of either victim's murder."

"That's true," I agreed. "But, we have reason to believe that she may have a sister who is seeking revenge for Juni's death."

If Jacob's eyebrows could rise any higher at my comment, they'd launch off his head. "Where did you get information that Juni has a sister?" His eyes narrowed at us.

"We aren't in a position to share that right now," Liz responded primly, and I glanced down to hide the laughter in my eyes. Even *she* didn't know where my information came from!

"What is the connection between this alleged sister and the second victim? If you're assuming she killed Roger because she believes Roger killed Juni, both very big ifs, by the way," he over-enunciated to make his point, "what possible reason could she have to kill Chad?"

"We don't know," I admitted, and Liz smacked me in the arm. "We don't," I reminded her, rubbing my upper arm. She packed a wallop.

"Anything else?" Jacob pointedly checked his watch.

"Nope, that's it. We just thought you should know," I finished lamely.

Jacob sighed. "No. Thank you. I'll make a note of it and let the FBI know when they arrive." His eyes appeared stricken the moment the words left his mouth. Or, more accurately, the initials.

Liz's eyes, however, lit up like it was her birthday. "The FBI is getting involved? Really?"

Jacob closed his eyes for a moment, knowing he couldn't retract his words. "Yes. That isn't public knowledge. You didn't hear it from me."

"Of course," I assured him, already worried what Liz might do with that information.

Liz extended her hand and Jacob clasped it, rather reluctantly it seemed to me. When their hands separated, he moved his in my direction. I reached out to shake goodbye.

A visible spark popped between us and then his hand enveloped mine. "Damn, that static electricity," I mumbled.

"Are you okay?" he murmured. His thumb rubbed my skin.

My cheeks flushed as heat flared in his eyes. How could we have this much attraction? I didn't even think he liked me.

Our hands separated and I answered, "I'm fine." I glanced at Liz, my heart sinking when I saw the smirk on her face. "We hope the information is helpful." I yanked the visitor badge lanyard over my head, Liz following suit, and flung them both at one of the volunteers.

I grabbed Liz's arm and steered her toward the glass door. I felt his eyes on me and despite my better judgment, risked a glance over my shoulder while we opened the door to exit. He had tilted his head, regarding me with another unreadable expression. I gave a half wave and scooted through the door before he had a chance to respond.

Liz wisely stayed silent until we were safely back in my car. "You two should just get a room," she crowed.

My cheeks flushed again. "I don't know what you mean."

"The heck you don't." She laughed. "There was a visible dang spark when you touched. Visible," she repeated. "That doesn't happen every day."

"Sure, it does," I argued. "It's called static electricity. Just like I explained to Jacob."

"Don't you mean Detective Dawson," she teased.

I sighed. "Whatever. We're done."

"What do you mean, we're done," she demanded, all trace of laughter gone.

I exited the parking lot onto Alta Drive, considered whether or not to take the 15 or surface roads back to the television station, while I deliberately delayed answering. Of course, I was going to continue to look into the murders. But, now that I knew for certain there was a paranormal aspect, I really didn't want a reporter of any kind involved. Too risky. Liz waited me out.

"We've given them a name. And now the FBI will be involved," I finally stated, not meeting the eyes I felt staring at me.

"Are you kidding? This is our story!"

"No, it's a probable serial killer," I countered. "And we are not the best people to solve it."

Liz stewed in her seat while I drove in the silence. I began to rethink my stance. Not about telling her about the paranormal underworld; I was for sure not breathing a word about that.

No, I was thinking about the adage, keep your enemies closer than your friends. Not that I considered Liz an enemy, but if I wanted to stay on top of what she was learning, continuing to work with her was the best way. What would be our next step that didn't involve the paranormal? I decided to pitch the question, sans the paranormal.

"What would be our next step then?"

"You'll keep investigating with me," she said excitedly. A twinge of guilt surfaced at my deception.

"Of course," I answered with a smile.

"Let's think a minute." Liz tapped her finger against her lip as she considered our next move. She jolted up in the seat, straining the seat belt. She faced me. "I know a tech guy; maybe he can do more with the partial picture of Juni. Also, I'll see what he can find on the dark web."

"Sounds like a plan," I agreed. "Since both victims were actors, I'll check in with friends of mine who know most of what's going on in Vegas." Liz eagerly agreed to our plan.

My mind raced. Technically, I'd already spoken to Catherine and Evie, but maybe they'd heard something new. Because I was actually stumped. I was fairly confident the murderer was the dead djinn's twin sister, but I was at a complete loss about how to find her. It'd been two days since Chad's murder and two weeks since Roger's murder. If she killed again, we probably had about ten days.

CHAPTER NINE

I was wrong about the ten days. I learned that when I reached out to Catherine the next morning. I chose the wrong day to sleep in.

"Did you see the news?!"

"Good morning to you too, Catherine," I answered with a laugh. "No, what did I miss?"

"There's been another murder!"

My good cheer died with her statement. "What happened?"

"In LA again, another actor," she explained. "My phone started blowing up before dawn. I'll bet Liz covers it on her show. It starts in ten minutes."

"I'll text you after the segment," I stated.

"Sounds good."

I ended the call and clicked the television on to wait for *Entertainment Daily* to begin. They teased the story in the show's intro and then broke for one set of commercials before presenting the meat of the story.

Liz looked good, in a fire-engine red sleeveless shift that fell decorously to her knees. With her four-inch Jimmy Choo's, she was captivating. Her eyes sparkled despite her somber expression and tone when she spoke.

"Details are scarce, and police aren't talking, but it appears the Firecracker Killer has struck again."

"Firecracker Killer?" I asked the air. "When did we start calling her that?"

"Last night, around midnight, another actor was killed while doing a Facebook Live video," she intoned. A graphic appeared with The Firecracker Killer in neon over a recorded video. My heart sank as I realized it was *the* video.

"Hi, everyone, for those of you who don't know me, I'm Bradley Reese," he introduced himself, setting off a set of cute dimples in his baby face. He couldn't be much more than twenty, with that mop of brown curls and smooth skin. The video paused as Liz continued to speak.

"And just like in the first two videos, Bradley realizes something isn't right."

Back to the video graphic. I closed my eyes, not wanting to see this baby die. Soon that part arrived.

"Do you hear that? What's that noise?" Bradley asked as popping sounds filled the space. And then silence.

"Police discovered the body after several viewers called 9-1-1," Liz told her own viewers. "Police have not used the expression *serial killer* yet." Though you now had, Liz. I was sure they appreciated that. "But, a source tells me—" Don't do it Liz! "—that the FBI has been called in to assist with the investigation. Maybe because the killer is crossing state lines? As a reminder, the first murder occurred in LA, the second here in the Valley, and the third now back in LA. We'll update you as we learn more information." Wide, toothy smile for the audience and then cut to commercial.

I sat back on my couch, thinking. At least she didn't disclose we thought an unidentified twin of a dead woman was the killer. That placated me a little. Liz sure did give up everything else. I knew Evie was getting her vampire sleep, but I grabbed my phone off the coffee table and texted Catherine.

Ugh. Come over?

Be right there.

About thirty minutes later, a knock on my door. I opened it immediately. Catherine looked paler than normal. I gave her a hug before stepping aside for her to enter my house.

On the way to the breakfast table, I paused at the refrigerator. "I know it's morning, but do you want a drink?"

Catherine laughed. "Yes, but I'm going to pass."

I figured she would. I just wanted to make her laugh. Mission accomplished. We settled into the wicker chairs. *Entertainment Daily* still played on the screen in the living room, but muted. "What do you think?"

"Honestly, I don't know." She stared out my sliding glass doors for a moment before turning to me. "I've told all my clients no more social media videos until the killer is caught."

"That sounds wise," I responded. "Why offer a target? Just for a little publicity."

"Exactly. Some of the younger ones who still believe they're invincible," she half-smiled at that, "tried to argue with me, but I made it clear. I will drop anybody who doesn't follow this order. And yes, it most definitely was an order," she answered my unasked question.

I nodded, unsmiling. "Good for you. They need to take this seriously. Especially since we don't know what Juni's sister wants."

"You're that certain it's the djinn's twin?"

"Yes. I am. That popping noise sealed the deal for me. There's really no other explanation. I just wish I had a motive."

Obviously hearing the frustration in my voice, Catherine gave my shoulder a squeeze. "You'll come up with something. What's next?"

I checked the time on my phone. "As soon as the show is over, I'm calling Liz. She has a friend working the digital angle to see if we can get anything. After that, we'll probably check in with Jacob again."

Catherine wasn't fast enough to hide her smile.

"What?"

"I find it interesting."

"Find what interesting?"

"You using Jacob's first name."

"So? We're friendly," I explained defensively. Why was I defensive?

"You light up when you say his name," she casually added.

My mouth dropped open. "I do not!"

She laughed openly now. "Yes, you do."

"I do?"

She nodded.

I sighed. "He's good looking, that's for sure," I admitted.

"That he is."

"Maybe when this is all over…" I stopped myself. "I don't think he even likes me. He treats me like a suspect!"

"That's just his nature," she explained. "There was definitely a spark. Literally."

"You don't know the half of it," I muttered and at her expression, filled her in on our second meeting.

"Well, then, I'd say there's definitely a spark!" She cackled at her own wit. We filled the rest of the time with idle chitchat until the show finished. The instant the show ended, I texted Liz. I didn't mention the FBI disclosure. I didn't like it, and I guessed Jacob didn't like it, but she was what she was.

Any new info?

Tech guy messaged. He's got news!!!! Wanna come get me?

On my way.

Catherine had been reading this over my shoulder and stood up at my final text. "Let me know if you need anything from me," she offered.

I gave her a hug at the door, told her to take it easy, and headed out to pick up Liz at the television station. I chuckled as I wondered if I'd ever see her actual home.

CHAPTER TEN

Liz stood tapping her foot when I drove up to get her. She hopped in before I'd even come to a complete stop.

"Good morning to you," I greeted her.

"I've already entered Chris's info into Google Maps. Just follow her instructions," she responded. "He's in Aliante," she added and I groaned. "Yeah, I know, but if I know my guy, it'll be worth it."

Aliante was at least a thirty minute drive from the television station. I stifled a response and simply hoped she was right about him being worth it.

"You caught the show." A statement, not a question.

"I did. How did you get the video so quickly? The murder was just last night."

"I have my sources."

Rolling my eyes, I stayed quiet. She jumped in to fill the silence.

"Okay, okay. Since the second murder, people have started taping when actors do Facebook Live videos. Quite a few people emailed me the video after the murder."

It was creepy how she sounded so cheerful. Another man died. Good grief.

"But, we really need new information. Chris is a genius online, so if he says he's got something, it's going to be good. I promise."

Her excitement was infectious and I smiled at her enthusiasm. "He didn't give you even the tiniest hint?"

"Nope, but that's Chris. He loves his drama," she laughed. I joined her; that was probably why they got along so well.

She scrolled through her cellphone. I drove in the silence while she checked whatever it was she was checking and soon we were pulling up to a two-story beige stucco house. It was virtually indistinguishable from half the homes in Vegas but appeared well-kept.

*****

A young man with smooth dark skin and dreadlocks opened the door with a wide smile.

"Hello, Liz and friend." He gave Liz a quick hug.

"Mia," I offered as we shook hands.

"Chris." He winked at me. "I can see by your expression that I do not fit your stereotype."

I reddened but acknowledged the remark.

"Unless you happen to live in the basement and this is really your mother's house," I quipped back and he belly laughed.

"Ah, but Mia, you know there are no basements in Vegas."

"Guest room?"

He laughed again. "No on both counts." He stepped aside to grant us entry. "Welcome to my humble abode. Although I will admit that I had interior decorating assistance."

"It clearly paid off," I responded and looked around. His home was beautifully appointed with matching earth-toned neutrals everywhere, a splash of red on throw pillows, and abstract art pieces on the walls.

"Thank you very much. Please, please, have a seat at the dining table." We gathered around a laptop on the table, chairs already thoughtfully arranged in a semicircle.

"Okay, let me show you what I found." Chris was all business once we were seated. "I don't know your technical background, so I'll go through all the steps," he said to me.

"Here's the picture that Liz gave me to start with," and the familiar image of Juni filled the screen. "As you know, image-detecting software doesn't work very well on partial images." He closed the image and opened up a new one. I gasped. "I know, right? I took your image and worked my magic to fill in what the other two thirds of her face looked like. I can't guarantee it, but I suspect this is pretty close."

Looking at the image of a front-facing Juni, I had to agree with him. If I saw the partial and this whole image side-by-side, I would be certain they were the same woman. Long brown hair. Dark, almost black eyes.

As if reading my mind, Chris hit a few keys and the partial popped up beside the full image rendering. I could see Liz nodding beside me.

"Dang, Chris. You are a genius."

"Thank you, Liz, but if that's all I could do, that wouldn't be as helpful, no?"

"True," she agreed with a chuckle.

"Good thing I did more." He closed those images and brought up a video, clearly showing the inside of a casino. "I ran a search for my new image. Nothing popped in criminal databases."

I opened my mouth to ask how he had access to those and closed it quickly. Not really my business.

"When I ran it against general photos and videos posted on the internet, well, that's when things got interesting." Without another word, he clicked start for the video. A cute couple, clearly inebriated, were talking to each other and the person holding the phone. Since they were obviously not Juni, I correctly assumed what I was looking for was in the background.

"Wait for it," Chris intoned and I leaned forward.

There! He hit the pause for the video just as a woman walked into frame behind the happy couple. Holy cow, it was definitely Juni. Chris waited for our reactions.

"Where is this, Chris?" Liz asked, her eyes squinting as she tried to see details that would disclose the location.

I realized why Chris was waiting. "*When* is this?" I asked instead and Chris nodded his approval.

"Exactly, Mia. The where is important, Liz, and it's at the Golden Nugget at Fremont. But, Mia hit the nail on the head. When I checked the time stamp for this video, it's a week ago."

To her credit, Liz instantly understood. "This is right before the murder. Well after Juni died," she exclaimed.

Chris nodded. "Yep, which makes things interesting. Either your girl Juni isn't dead, or this is the twin sister you're looking for."

My head was spinning. If I was wrong about Juni being a djinn, then this very well could be Juni and she likely was our murderer. If I was right about Juni being a djinn, then this was likely her twin sister who was our murderer. But, if this was Juni, what was her motive for murder? Angry at Roger for some reason. But why kill the others? And if it was the twin sister, I was still back to my question of her motive for the murders of Chad and Bradley…too many ifs. I realized Liz and Chris were staring at me.

"What are you thinking?" Liz asked.

"Did you find her on any of the security footage at the Golden Nugget?"

"I may have access to certain private databases," he coyly answered, "but even I cannot access casino security footage. And I don't know anybody who would give me access. Do you?" This last directed at Liz.

She frowned while she thought. "Not at the Golden Nugget."

"No other videos popped with her image?" I asked Chris.

"I'm afraid not."

I winked at them both. "Then it looks like we're heading to Fremont!"

CHAPTER ELEVEN

Fremont used to have so much free parking, I lamented before I pulled over to my usual metered spot. Whenever I headed to Fremont, I kept it simple and grabbed a metered spot on Sixth Street. I was usually only a couple of blocks from anywhere I wanted to go in the area. I fed $4 to the meter. That should buy us enough time.

Liz and I walked to the Fremont Street Experience, which housed the Golden Nugget Hotel & Casino, among many other colorful attractions. Sometimes it was best to avert your gaze! I totally understood making a living, but I didn't really need to see a middle-aged man with a beer gut wearing an American flag bikini. Liz and I heard a thumping beat and saw a small crowd gathered around one of the street artists. Liz rolled her eyes when I pulled her closer.

"Really, Mia? How long have you lived in Vegas?"

"I like the dancing," I confessed. We peeked around the edge of the crowd. "Dang." No dancers. Just a guy doing a card trick. Probably a pretty good one, with the crowd he attracted, but still. I usually only stopped for the dancers. They reminded me of the movements of underwater creatures so close to my heart.

We continued past the card dealer. Past the man spray painted silver standing statue still. Past the woman sitting cross legged on the concrete playing a flute. Past the two women wearing showgirl outfits calling out to the men, "Take a picture with a showgirl!" I admired the elaborate red and blue headdresses of the women but carefully avoided eye contact. They usually tried for the guys, but making eye contact with any of the street artists increased the likelihood of engagement, and some of them could be pretty darn aggressive. And we had neither the time nor the interest in engaging. But I wished them lots of luck with the tourists.

Liz and I reached the Golden Nugget Hotel & Casino. We stared up at the entrance. It wasn't quite as impressive during the day as it was all lit up at night, but the gold-lined rounded cover over the entrance and the faux-gold plating on the exterior walls were still pretty sparkly. I was thankful that I didn't require breathing to survive when we entered the casino. It was midday so not quite as bad as it would be in the evening, but the smoke crawled over my skin. Liz coughed and grimaced.

"Ugh," was all she said but I understood.

We stepped off to the side just inside the door to get our bearings. It was a casino; lots of flashing lights and random jingles coming off the various slot machines. Casinos made most of their money off the slot machines; something I'd never really understood. You had zero control over the outcome. It was 100% luck if you won. At least with the table games, if you had skill, you could tilt the odds a little bit. I internally shrugged. I didn't gamble, so to each their own.

"Now we find a security guard," I stated, searching the floor for one.

"There!" Liz pointed over toward the far end of the space, where a man stood impassively like an endcap on the row of slots. We approached him, side stepping the tourists in their shorts and flip flops, holding either cameras or alcoholic beverages, rarely both.

"What's our story?" Liz asked.

"I'm not sure," I admitted. "But, I'm fairly certain this guy won't be able to help us. We need his boss."

"Good point. Let's just ask for him."

We'd reached the security guard. "How can I help you?" he asked, courteously, if clearly by rote.

Liz gave him her biggest smile. "We'd like to talk to the head of security, please." The guard's eyes narrowed and he looked closer at the two of us.

"Maybe I could help you…"

"We'd rather discuss it with him," she demurred.

The guard stared down at us for a beat and then understanding dawned in his eyes. "I know you," he said, almost but not quite accusatory.

"Well," Liz responded, looking down and fluttering her lashes. I just barely managed not to laugh at her fake-coy routine. Oh brother.

Now the guard was excited. "You're Elizabeth Addison! From that morning show."

Liz held up her hands. "You got me."

The guard lowered his voice. "Is this about a story?"

Leaning in to whisper, matching his tone, Liz answered, "I can't confirm or deny that." Then she winked.

"For you, Ms. Addison, I'll get Mr. Maliton. But, I'll be honest. He's probably not going to want to help," the guard warned us.

"That's okay," she assured him. "If you can get him, we'll take it from there."

We could definitely take it from there.

CHAPTER TWELVE

The guard spoke into a walkie talkie, requesting Mr. Maliton to the floor.

A few minutes later, a slim man in a gangster business suit approached. He looked like he got lost in the 1940s. If I'd been drinking anything, I might have shot it out my nose.

"Johnny, what can I help with?" Mr. Maliton directed the question at the guard, with a quick flick of a glance at the two of us.

"The ladies requested to see you, sir," Johnny responded, keeping it simple. Smart.

Mr. Maliton looked like he wanted to say something more to Johnny, probably about the complete lack of information contained in that statement. He thought better of it, and addressed us instead.

"What can I help you ladies with?"

He nodded at Johnny, who moved away discretely.

Liz smiled at the security head. "We'd like to take a look at your security cameras," she requested with complete confidence. Unfortunately, the bold approach failed.

"I'm afraid that's not possible," Mr. Maliton responded.

"Let's start over," she replied, sticking out her hand. "I'm Elizabeth Addison, with *Entertainment Daily*." Although the security head accepted her offered hand, inwardly I cringed. I watched the screen drop over his eyes. She lost him and didn't even know it yet.

"It's a pleasure to meet you, Ms. Addison," he politely stated. "You still can't see the security footage. Company policy."

Liz tried to ply her feminine wiles on the man, since playing the media card didn't work. I tuned them both out. I needed a distraction for Liz so I could entrance Mr. Maliton. A glance around the casino floor found nothing that could help. Screw it.

"Mr. Maliton?" I directed the question squarely at the security head and watched as his eyes took on the familiar glazed expression.

"Yes?"

"We understand that it's company policy, and we certainly wouldn't want you to get in trouble," I explained, hoping Liz wasn't being impacted too much.

My voice entranced anyone within earshot, to some degree.

"Thank you, I appreciate that," he said in a monotone.

"But, we really need to see that security footage."

He frowned, his training fighting the sound of my voice. He'd lose, so I waited.

"Okay."

"Thank you." I touched his arm and he smiled at me. I risked a glance at Liz, confirmed by her eyes that unfortunately, she'd been entranced too.

"Can we see them now?"

"Of course," he agreed and walked away.

"Come on, Liz," I said, and she followed along too.

Our little train made its way through the casino floor to a room off a short hallway. It looked like a scene out of a movie. A man sat before a bank of television screens, each of which clearly showed sections of the casino floor. The man appeared surprised to see Mr. Maliton at all, let alone trailed by two women. He jumped to his feet.

"Good afternoon, Mr. Maliton," he spluttered.

"These ladies need to see some security footage, Rick."

Rick gaped at Mr. Maliton and then us. "Sir?" As if maybe he didn't hear him correctly.

"Please show them whatever they need."

"But, sir?"

"Is something about what I've said unclear?" Mr. Maliton's voice, despite still sounding soft and sleepy, registered with Rick.

"No, sir," he replied smartly.

"Thank you, Mr. Maliton," I said with a final touch of his arm. "We'll take it from here." Rick's eyes bugged out at this exchange, especially when his boss nodded at us and walked out of the room.

"Hi, Rick," I said with a little wave. Out of the corner of my eye, I saw Liz give a small shake of her head now that the entrancement was broken. I resolutely did not look at her and focused on our new best friend, Rick.

"Thank you in advance for all your help."

"Uh, sure. What do you need?" His thoughts were clearly telegraphed on his face: Who is this green-haired chick and why did my boss give her carte blanche? I managed not to laugh.

"We need to go back about a week," I explained, showing him the time stamp on the image Chris gave us. "The camera that shows this angle, looking for the woman in the background."

Rick stared back and forth between the image and his cameras, working out which one would show that view.

"Aha!" He pointed to a screen on his right. I compared the two and nodded my agreement. He spun in his chair to a computer behind him, began typing away.

"Give me a sec, and I'll find that spot," he called over his shoulder. I watched as images fast forwarded, rewound, while he looked for this exact moment. And then there she was. Our mystery woman. Rick saw her and hit pause.

"There's your image. Now what?"

Liz, who seemed to have fully shaken off the entrancement, chimed in. "Let's go backwards until she leaves frame, so we can see where she entered. We'll track her movements."

Rick nodded his understanding and we began what I thought would be a painstaking process of tracking the mystery woman throughout the casino. Except that it wasn't, because we couldn't.

"That's weird," Rick muttered. We re-watched.

The three of us could clearly see the woman in one frame, but she was absent on any frame prior. It was as if she had just popped into existence. And then she was in about twenty seconds of frame before she seemingly vanished again.

We watched this twenty second clip over and over; Rick even checked other cameras at that time, to see if she was in any other footage. She was not. We were baffled. The other two tried to figure out how she could appear and disappear like she seemed to.

"Camera failure," was Rick's explanation, though he didn't sound like he really believed. And he shouldn't. I knew he was wrong; this was enough additional confirmation for me that the mystery woman was a djinn.

The reason I was baffled right along with the other two was wanting to know why. Why was Juni/Twin Sister appearing at all?

"Oh my goodness!" I exclaimed when I finally saw it. The other two jumped at my exhalation.

"What?" Liz cried.

"Rick, back the video up ten seconds." He complied. "There! Do you see him?" Rick and Liz followed my finger. Rick didn't know who I was looking at, but Liz did.

"Is that Chad?"

"Yes," I confirmed, staring at the dead lead in my film, looking very much alive. Our mystery woman was staring at him, and although her face was expressionless, it was clear he was her target.

"Rick," I turned to our helpful security agent. "Can you make me a copy of this twenty seconds of coverage?"

"Of course," he readily agreed. He was still obviously confused, but Mr. Maliton had made it super clear that we were to get whatever we wanted. I hid a smile.

"Thank you."

I turned to Liz while he made the copy. "Now we have at least a visual connection between Chad and the mystery woman."

"Is this where she first meets him?"

"That's a good question. She doesn't interact with him at all that we see, but it seems evident that she's tracking him. Does that suggest to you that she was looking for him? Already knew him somehow?"

Liz followed my line of questions. "What if she already identified him somehow and now wanted to…what?"

"I don't know," I admitted. "Let's get a copy of this to Jacob. Maybe he and the FBI will know more." I saw Rick's ears perk up at those initials and I regretted stating that in front of him. Oh well, who was he gonna tell?

Rick handed me a flash drive. "Here's the video." I knew he was dying to ask questions, but he admirably restrained himself.

"Thank you very much, Rick," I said. "You've been a big help."

Liz and I left the security guard at his post, monitoring the camera feeds, and returned to my car.

CHAPTER THIRTEEN

Liz suggested going back to the station to download the clip to her work computer, where we could then more easily share it with Selina and Jacob. I bit my tongue at what I was sure was her real reason: making sure she had a copy for herself.

"You aren't going to air this yet, are you?" I finally just asked her.

"Not yet."

I guessed that'd have to do. While I drove to the station, Liz texted Selina to inform her the video would be coming. Once we arrived at the station, I texted Jacob asking to meet.

"You know, you could just email him the video," Liz teased after I told her who I was texting.

"I'd like the opportunity to talk to him," I responded casually but she wasn't buying.

"Just admit you like him and want to see him."

We were sitting in her office now, door firmly closed. I took this time to analyze my fingernails, saw that a manicure would be nice. Had I ever gotten a manicure before? Surely, though honestly, I didn't recall.

Liz laughed at my silence. "Fine, ignore me. That was pretty cool, what you did," she changed the subject.

"What are you talking about?" I knew what she was talking about.

"Convincing the head of security to show us the security footage. How did you do that exactly?" She was still going for light and easy, but I heard the undercurrent.

"I just explained that we needed it," I reminded her. "You were there. You heard me."

"Yeah, I did," she agreed, but when I glanced up from my nails, she was frowning. "It's kind of fuzzy though."

"Fuzzy? I don't get it," I stated the bold lie, but not really feeling guilty.

"Listening to your voice was quite musical. I never noticed that before."

"Hmm, thanks?"

"It's almost like—"

Our eyes met. "Like what?"

"I'm not sure." Big smile blossomed; totally fake, but I was okay with that. "Never mind," she finally stated, "at least we got what we needed."

I breathed a slight sigh of relief that she let it go. It wasn't good that her antennae were up and twitching, but it was worth the risk.

Liz focused on her screen, transferring the video from the flash drive to her computer. While she finished that and sent the email to Selina, my phone pinged an incoming text. "Jacob?" she asked and I nodded.

"He says he can meet in an hour. Did you want to come?"

The universe heard my unspoken request when Liz shook her head no. "I'm going to wrap a few things up here, including sending this video to Chris for his input; maybe we can meet up later at your place for drinks and catch up on our progress?"

"Sure," I agreed.

"I'll see you tonight," Liz commented with a quick glance at me.

Guess I'd been dismissed.

CHAPTER FOURTEEN

Jacob apparently convinced his higher ups that being in training while there was now a serial killer bouncing back and forth between LA and Las Vegas was not a good idea. He asked if we could meet at a fast-casual restaurant in Downtown Summerlin. They had a great pizza place there, so I readily agreed. Since I had an hour, I popped by my condo to transfer the video file to my laptop before heading to meet him.

I turned off of Sahara Ave onto a road that wrapped around the open-air shopping center behemoth. Luckily, my destination was a little off to the side, where there was usually ample close parking. I grabbed a spot and headed for the restaurant. Jacob was already sitting at a patio table. My heart skipped a beat. The sun reflected off his blond hair and I could see his broad shoulders straining the threads of his gray t-shirt.

Not to admit that Liz was right, but I really was glad that it was just me and Jacob at this meeting.

He looked up at the sound of my footsteps and smiled when he saw me.

"Hi, Ms. Fynn," he said as he stood.

"Didn't I ask you to call me Mia?"

"Hi, Mia."

"Hi, Jacob."

We stood staring at each other with matching grins. Like teenagers. I broke the moment first.

"You ready to head inside?"

He indicated I should go first, though he was careful to open the pizzeria door for me. I ducked under his arm and he followed me. We made idle chit chat about traffic and the weather as we placed our orders. He paid for my food, despite my stating it wasn't necessary. This wasn't a date, I reminded myself, though I didn't say that to Jacob.

We sat at an outside table for more privacy and to enjoy the beautiful sunny day. I handed him the flash drive with the video.

"I figured you might want the original copy," I said by way of explanation for not simply emailing it. Not terribly logical, since it was already a copy, but Jacob didn't challenge my statement.

"Thanks. Can you tell me more about what's on it?"

All I had texted was that I had a video showing the possible murderer. I skipped the background information involving Chris. "We saw a clip of a woman on an iPhone video from someone who had been on vacation here. We figured out where that video was taken and went there. We then found security footage—" Here Jacob lifted one eyebrow. I continued.

"Footage that showed that same location and time. And there she was. More importantly, there was Chad."

Jacob whistled low in appreciation. "You actually found a video showing this unidentified woman and the murder vic?"

I nodded, inordinately proud of myself. "Yes, it clearly shows her looking at him."

"Really? That's interesting. I'll watch the video in a second, but since you seem to have deliberately not mentioned it, where did you get this video?" He was smirking, so I knew he was teasing, but I tensed and he noticed.

"Hey, what's wrong?"

I shook my head. "Nothing, sorry. The video is from the Golden Nugget."

Now both of his eyebrows shot up. "You successfully got security footage from a casino? Without a search warrant? What did you do? Bribe them?" He was still joking, but there was definitely an edge.

"Of course not!" I exclaimed. "Although honestly, I wouldn't have had a problem doing that," I admitted. "I just asked nicely."

"Okay." He stared at me while I strove for a carefully neutral expression. He sighed. "I'll accept that."

"I thought maybe between the department's and the FBI's resources, you guys could do more with the video. The date and time on it correspond to shortly before the murder. It seems highly unlikely that it's not connected."

"Based on your description, I would tend to agree. Okay, let's fire it up."

Jacob remained silent while he watched the twenty second clip on my laptop. He hit play several more times. I was acutely aware of the heat of his body so close to mine as we leaned in toward the screen.

"Is this it?" he finally asked, confusion apparent in his voice.

"What do you mean? Yes, that's it." I pointed at the screen.

"Where does she come from and where does she go?" He asked this slowly.

I sighed. "Oh, that. Yeah, we don't know."

"You don't know? Did your source not check the other cameras?"

"Yes! He did. I was standing right there when he did. She's not on any of the other cameras."

"That's not possible."

Not if you're not human. "Security guy said there must have been a camera malfunction."

Jacob stared at me for a moment.

"More like a system malfunction."

"That's possible too," I conceded, hating lying to him. But what was I going to say? She was a djinn who popped in and out of our dimension. Not a chance.

"What are you thinking?"

"What?"

"Just now, I saw the wheels in your brain turning," he explained. "What were you thinking?"

Um. I tried for a version of the truth. "I'm trying to figure out why she was there."

"And you think this is Juni's sister, not Juni, even though no body was ever found?" He asked but really this was a dismissive statement.

"I do," I answered.

"Why?"

Now what did I say? "I just think that since the first murder victim was so adamant that Juni was in his car and nobody's seen her since that night—"

"Except possibly on this video," he interrupted.

"It seems more likely that it would be somebody connected to her," I continued as though he didn't speak.

"And somehow decided there must be a sister. Apparently, a twin sister," he amended with a gesture at the video paused on the mystery woman. "How did you come across this information?"

"Sources," I stated firmly. "Sources that I will not be providing to you, so please don't ask again."

Jacob looked taken aback by my tone but didn't push. "Since you provided the initial direction, I feel comfortable telling you that so far we have not been able to identify this woman further. Therefore, we have not been able to identify any family members, twin or otherwise." He paused to take in my reaction. "Therefore," he repeated, "it appears you have better sources than Metro or the FBI."

I heard the exasperation in his voice and wished I could help him. "I'm sorry I can't help more," I said instead.

We stared at each other. He started to say something several times but didn't. I waited. I didn't know what else to tell him that didn't put my kind at risk. I was however disappointed to hear his report. Liz and I were going to have to solve this ourselves. Without Liz learning the real truth. I sighed before I could stop myself.

Jacob misinterpreted the sigh. "No, I'm sorry. I don't mean to pressure you. I understand protecting sources. I just want to solve this before anyone else gets hurt." The naked worry I saw in his eyes threatened my resolve, but I held steady.

I reached out to cover his hand with my own. The familiar zap of electricity brought smiles to both our faces. "I guess that's going to keep happening." I chuckled but didn't move my hand, nor did he withdraw his.

"It's okay, Jacob," I assured him. "I know you're just trying to do your job. I'm sorry I can't help more," I repeated.

Jacob squeezed my hand, sending pleasurable shock waves through my body. "I appreciate everything you're trying to do. Even if you're hanging out with the press."

We both laughed and the moment was broken. Our hands separated and we gathered up the trash from our lunch. Jacob walked me to my car.

This was not a date, I kept reminding myself.

His look of uncertainty when we reached my car had me wondering if he was experiencing the same indecision. He brushed his fingers across my cheek, surprising us both with the action and the small spark.

"I guess I'll need to be more careful when I touch you," he said softly. My lips ached for him to kiss me, but he took a step back and shook his head. "Apologies, this is neither the time nor the place."

"No apologies necessary," I responded.

He smiled and turned to walk away. I focused on the words he spoke. If this wasn't the time or place, that suggested some other time or place would be right. I was disconcerted by how happy the thought made me.

CHAPTER FIFTEEN

I texted Catherine and Evie to meet me when the sun set; Catherine texted back immediately confirming, and I knew Evie would respond when she awoke. It was only mid-afternoon, so I had several hours to kill. I decided to conduct more of my own research to see what I could find. With a glass of Riesling in one hand and my laptop in the other, I made myself comfortable on the bleached wood Adirondack chair on my patio and dove in.

A knock at my door startled me. I realized it must be my ladies arriving. I couldn't believe I completely lost track of time.

"Coming!" I called out, though it was uncertain I could be heard through the door. I closed the sliding glass door behind me, set down my laptop and empty glass on my dining table, and headed to see which of my expected visitors had arrived.

"Did you forget I was coming?"

"Liz! Of course not. What time is it?" I made a show of checking my watch. "Did you text me you were on your way?"

She appeared genuinely contrite and I felt guilty for being rude. After all, we did have plans; it wasn't her fault I forgot. I just knew that her presence would alter how the evening went. Catherine appeared behind Liz.

"Hey, Mia," Catherine said to me but looking at Liz.

"Hi, I'm Liz," she introduced herself, hand outstretched.

"Catherine," she responded to Liz.

"Right. Where are my manners? Please, come in. We have one more coming." I moved to allow them entrance.

"I didn't know it was a party," Liz called over her shoulder.

Catherine stared at me and I shrugged. We would keep it brief and then have our paranormal conversation after Liz left.

As I was closing the door, three sharp knocks sounded. I pulled it back open to see Evie's smiling face.

"Hey, Mia," she said and we hugged.

"We have another guest," I said in a low voice and felt her shift to see around me. We released the hug and she followed me in.

Liz and Catherine were already seated at the dining table. I introduced Evie to Liz and she joined the ladies.

"Drinks?"

"None for me," Evie declined my offer with a smirk that piqued the interest of Liz. I inwardly rolled my eyes. Thanks, Evie.

"I'll take whatever wine was previously in this glass," Liz accepted my offer.

"Same," Catherine chimed in.

Although Catherine and Evie recognized Liz, she briefly explained who she was and they reciprocated with the basics. I joined them at the table with the wine.

"I brought another bottle."

"Excellent," Catherine responded.

"Okay, now that we're all here," I began. "Let's talk about the murders."

Liz glanced between Evie and Catherine.

"They both knew Chad," I offered as explanation for their presence. "They helped me figure out that Juni has a twin sister."

"The more the merrier," Liz responded blithely, but I saw her immediate interest when I disclosed them as the source of our biggest piece of information. I was probably going to regret telling her that.

I brought Evie and Catherine up to speed regarding the security footage and then summarized my quick lunch with Jacob. I blatantly ignored Evie's and Catherine's reactions to learning that I had lunch with Jacob, but Liz didn't.

"She totally likes him, am I right?"

Evie guffawed and Catherine actually snort-laughed. "Oh yeah," they agreed.

"Thanks ladies, but who I may or may not like is not the focus of this meeting," I reminded them, which just sent them into hysterics. "Why is this so funny?"

"Because you both clearly like each other and it's funny watching you dance around that," Liz said bluntly. I was undecided whether I liked this personality trait.

"Anyway," I said to bring them back on track. "What do we think?"

The three women were quiet. Frankly, we were all at a bit of a loss.

"If only we knew where she was going to be," Catherine said offhand with a small chuckle.

"That's it!"

"What's it, Liz?" I asked.

"We need to know where she's going to be," she explained, and we stared at her. "We need to bait her."

"This isn't a movie," Catherine responded.

"I think it has merit," Evie disagreed. "What do you think, Mia?"

I slowly nodded my head. "Catherine's right that it's not a movie. On the other hand, Evie has a point too."

"Do you like the idea or not?" Liz asked.

I laughed. "Like? I don't know about that! But, I think it's probably our best bet."

Catherine frowned and I hurried to continue.

"Look at it this way. Based on her pattern, she's likely going to kill again within a day or two. Even with the additional information we've given law enforcement, I doubt they'll find her before another murder occurs." I didn't add that as a djinn, law enforcement almost certainly would be unable to capture her; and unless they surprised her and shot her through the heart, they weren't going to kill her either.

"Okay, what do you guys have in mind?" Catherine asked.

"What do we know about her pattern?" Evie answered a question with a question.

"She's picked actors all three times," I began. "And she's alternated between here and LA. Our best bet is an actor here in town, since the third murder was in LA."

The women nodded.

"I wouldn't feel right about putting an actor at risk," Evie objected.

"We could bring the police in on our plan; maybe they could use an undercover officer as a fake actor?"

"I have a better idea, Catherine," Liz said.

We looked at her expectantly.

"I'm going to do it."

"What? What are you talking about? You're not an actor. Or male," I argued, pointing out the gender preference of our killer.

"Look at it logically. Even if we have an undercover officer, how are we going to get Juni or her twin sister to pick him as the next victim? We have to bring her to us."

"True, but whatever you're going to do, an undercover officer could probably do," Catherine argued.

Liz was shaking her head. "No, he can't. Our hypothetical undercover officer doesn't have a television show."

"That's good," Catherine reluctantly admitted.

"Even if she doesn't watch the show, if I say I want to interview her, that's gonna go viral on social media within thirty minutes. I can practically guarantee it," she crowed.

"I think she's right," I agreed.

"And we can still have the police involved for additional protection," Catherine mused.

Believe it or not, as much as the ladies were right about me wanting to see Jacob, I didn't think bringing the police in for our plan made sense since they couldn't do anything to the djinn. Except I couldn't explain that right now without telling Liz everything about the paranormal underworld. Instead, I nodded at her.

"I'll call Jacob."

CHAPTER SIXTEEN

"Are you women insane?" As predicted, Jacob didn't like our plan. He sat at my dining table, staring at me, Liz, Catherine, and Evie like we'd all sprouted second heads. "This is a terrible idea and there's no way Metro will support it."

"Technically, Detective, as a free citizen, you can't stop me from going on my own show and asking her for an interview," Liz countered sweetly. "We've informed you of the plan and you can either participate or not."

If the tension radiating off of him were physical, it would knock Liz on her bottom. He looked at each of us in turn. "Surely you realize this won't work," he tried another tack.

"Why not?" Evie asked.

"Once you announce on air and all over social media what you're doing, every Tom, Dick, and Harry is going to camp out in front of your house. She's never going to show with the circus in town."

Liz frowned. That had obviously not occurred to her. She brightened. "I disagree. What is it that law enforcement says about so many serial killers? They want to brag about what they've done. They want people to recognize their brilliance. They want to tell their stories. Right?"

"True. But how is she supposed to get to your home, if it's surrounded by the press and the curious?"

"Well, Detective, I live in a gated community, so that'll cut down some."

Jacob snorted. "Please. Those gates won't hold anybody out. Besides, won't that keep her out too?"

"Look, maybe you're right. But this is a woman who has been able to get in and out of locked homes without breaking anything or leaving any forensic evidence behind. I have no doubt that with the proper motivation, she'll figure her way around the gate, press, and the lookie loos." She shrugged. "I'm not worried."

"There's nothing I can say that will talk you out of this." We shook our heads no. He sighed. "Fine. I'll talk to my superiors. I doubt they'll spare more than an officer or two for what they'll consider a farce. I'll be there, of course." Our eyes briefly met and I smiled.

We reviewed the details and decided to put our plan into motion the next morning. After the group departed,

I moved to my couch with my third glass of wine. I hoped we were doing the right thing.

*****

"Good morning in the Valley!" Liz welcomed viewers to *Entertainment Daily* with a toothy smile and a fabulous form-fitting red dress and stiletto heels. Her smile dimmed.

"As viewers of this show know, the so-called Firecracker Killer has murdered three actors in as many weeks – Bradley Reese, Roger Miller, and Chad Johnson. These murders in Las Vegas and Los Angeles have set the West Coast entertainment world on edge, with promoters warning their clients not to use social media for streaming, and both local law enforcement and the FBI coming up empty."

Liz breathed deeply. Genuine nerves or for show? I honestly didn't know.

"Today, I'd like to formally invite the Firecracker Killer to come to my home, tonight, for me to interview during a Facebook Live video." She stared into the camera. "I know you have a story to tell. Let me help you tell it."

She turned to another camera, smiled. "What big charity event is in the works for the Valley? We'll tell you after the break."

The show cut to commercial and I sat back in awe. She did it. She actually asked a serial killer into her home.

*****

Time crawled while I waited for it to be time to watch Liz interview a serial killer. Just as I made up my mind to take a quick swim in the pool to burn off some nervous energy, someone knocked on my front door. I hadn't ordered anything online, and I lived in a gated community. I debated ignoring the knock but curiosity got the better of me. My jaw dropped when I saw the woman standing before me.

"Councilwoman Knollman? What an unexpected surprise," I squeaked out.

"Good afternoon, Ms. Fynn," Barbara Knollman, Las Vegas's resident demon councilwoman, addressed me formally.

"May I come in?"

I hesitated and irritation flashed in her eyes. "Of course," I agreed, stepping aside to allow her entry. Rumor said Barbara was a fairly laidback demon, but still. A demon. In my home. I shuddered as I closed the door behind her.

Barbara took several steps inside before turning to face me. "This is fine. I won't be here long."

"Why are you here?"

"I saw Ms. Addison's show this morning."

"Ah, yes. It was something," I hedged, wondering at her interest in the murders. Did she know something about the djinn?

"Something, indeed," Barbara agreed. "I understand you're working with her."

A statement, not a question. I didn't bother to wonder how she knew. She had moles everywhere. "Yes."

"What else does she know?"

"I don't understand the question."

"It wasn't complex. What else does she know besides what she reported in the broadcast?"

It hit me what she was asking. "Nothing about us," I assured the demon. If Barbara decided Liz was a threat, well, that wouldn't do much for Liz's lifespan. The brief look of disappointment on Barbara's face surprised me. Did she want Liz to know about us? Frankly, this was why I stayed out of paranormal politics.

"Did you know that I have precognitive abilities?"

Now my jaw really did drop open. "Um, I did not," I answered, my mind swirling.

"I share this because I want you to understand the importance of what I'm about to tell you," she explained. "You are on the right track."

"I am?"

"You are. Do not be swayed from it."

"Okay. Wait," I paused, thinking furiously, "which part? Helping Liz, keeping things from her, pursuing the killer?"

"I've said what I came to say," she responded, ignoring my questions.

Before I could try asking another way, she turned. "I'll see myself out."

And with that, she was gone.

CHAPTER SEVENTEEN

"How do I look?" Liz asked me this, spinning in a circle. "I'm going for upscale casual." She smoothed out nonexistent wrinkles on her violet nylon shift.

"You look great," I told her, amazed that she was concerned about her appearance at all. I finally got to see her house. It was a cute two-story in a gated country club neighborhood. On a tiny lot, however, so set-up was a challenge. Liz and I were the only ones in her home; we were currently in her home office.

She stood in front of a mid-size dark wood desk. Certificates and framed photos with famous folks dotted the walls. Unfortunately, the office was on the street-facing side of the home. Despite the gate, as Jacob had predicted, cars lined the street. People sat waiting in most of them. I idly wondered how many were press versus the curious.

Jacob and two officers commandeered the house next door, their cars safely hidden in the garage, the owners' vehicles relegated to the street. Catherine and Evie were with them. We'd been texting fast and furious while the time passed. I'd already updated them on the way weird visit from the demon councilwoman. They were as much at a loss as I was.

All three of the times of death were after the standard dinner hour and before midnight. The sun set about an hour ago, so it was almost time. The energy in the air crackled. I both wanted and didn't want Juni's twin sister to make an appearance. I hadn't told the others my actual plan.

A text notification vibrated my phone. Jacob.

"It's go time," I relayed to Liz, who moved behind the desk. I vacated the room. She logged on to Facebook and prepared to start streaming.

I watched the start of the Facebook Live video on my cellphone in a darkened room at the back of the house. There had been some concern that my presence in the home might keep the murderer from showing. Nobody really wanted Liz to be alone, though, so hiding in the back seemed the best option. My phone was on silent. I could hear the faintest hint of what she was saying from the other room.

Nothing happened and Liz started to repeat herself. "I'm here in my home, waiting on the appearance of the

Firecracker Killer. So far, he or she has not appeared." I was glad she decided not to use the feminine pronoun. I didn't think the police would want us to inform the world that we suspected the killer was female.

The random chatter on the video continued; I watched the comments scrolling by. They alternated between people calling Liz crazy for trying this or an idiot because the killer wouldn't show with such a contrived scene.

It looked like the latter were right.

Time stretched on and the comments slacked off. Ninety minutes into the now terminally boring video, Jacob texted me.

I'm calling it. She's not coming.

I'll let Liz know.

She was going to be disappointed. She'd been so excited about this plan. Standing in the doorway of the office, I made the universal slicing motion across my throat. *Kill it.* Liz subtly shook her head and continued speaking.

I texted this response to Jacob. I remained standing in the doorway for another five minutes before Liz accepted reality.

"Well, folks, it looks like the Firecracker Killer doesn't want to tell his or her story tonight. I'm signing off. Until next time." She gave a half-hearted smile and finally killed the stream.

"Dammit!" She pounded her fist on the desk, rattling pens in a yellow plastic cup with the MnM logo on the side. She ran a hand through her brunette curls. "That sucks."

I walked to the window and, peering through the blinds, watched the few remaining cars peel away. We heard the front door open.

"Ms. Addison, it's Detective Dawson."

"In the office."

Jacob, Catherine, and Evie entered the room a moment later and we stood silently.

"Guess you were right."

"I wish I wasn't," Jacob countered Liz's statement. She looked past the trio to the empty doorway.

"Where are the officers?"

"I sent them home."

"I see."

I watched this awkward exchange like a tennis match. Now what?

"I'm going to head back to the station to write up a quick report of the evening's activities."

"Or lack thereof," Liz added. "It's okay, you can say it."

"I'll be in touch." He turned to me at the window. "Mia, can I talk to you a minute?" My heart fluttered. I followed him from the room, resolutely ignoring the knowing expressions on the ladies' faces.

"Now that you're out of the investigation," Jacob started, and I didn't bother to correct his incorrect assumption, "I was wondering." He stalled.

"Wondering what, Jacob?"

He stared at the ground. "Would you like to have dinner with me?" he asked in a rush.

"A date?"

His cheeks reddened at my question. "Yes, a date."

"I would love to," I answered and our dopey smiles mirrored each other.

"Okay, I'll call you tomorrow."

"Sounds good." I reached my hand out, then withdrew it, wondering if I should hug him. But he was out the door before I'd made a decision. Guess neither one of us dated much!

Giggling greeted me as I reentered the office. There was no need to ask if they overheard.

"Mia and Jacob, sitting in a tree, K-I-S-S-I-N-G," Liz sang. The other two practically fell over laughing.

"Very mature, guys," I responded, but my ear-to-ear grin betrayed me. "Anyway, we'll get out of your hair. Come on, ladies."

Liz closed the door behind us.

Catherine and Evie took but a step before they stopped and faced me.

"What do you think?" Evie asked.

"I'm not sure."

"Do you think she didn't come because of the crowd?" Catherine asked.

"I don't think so. Since she can appear and disappear at will, the crowd wouldn't really have been a factor, I don't think."

"You think she just didn't want to be interviewed?" Evie asked.

"That's more likely," I acknowledged. "She's an immortal being. Whatever her reason for killing men like this, she's been around long enough to see technology as the blip that it is. Plus," I paused.

"What?" Catherine asked.

"It's unusual for a djinn to act this way – it's not unknown for them to kill, of course, but so publicly?" I shrugged.

Evie nodded in agreement. "You think maybe she's not thinking straight, that something's really wrong?"

"Yeah. I had hoped that she'd come tonight, so we could end this," I said vaguely. "But if she's not thinking clearly or logically, then all bets are off."

CHAPTER EIGHTEEN

The next morning dawned with a sense of foreboding and I wasn't sure why. A couple of scrambled eggs and a cup of coffee later, I turned on the television to see how Liz handled what happened last night. She seemed to shake off the disappointment well enough by the time we left.

"Good morning in the Valley!" Liz began with her normal greeting, again looking chic in a pink halter dress ending just above her knees.

"Thank you to those who tuned in last night to my Facebook Live attempt to interview the Firecracker Killer. If you watched, then you know that unfortunately, he or she did not show up for the interview." Fake laugh. Guess she hadn't let it go yet.

"Here's the thing, everybody. This is too important to let go. So, I'm not." Her eyes glittered. "Let's go again, Firecracker. I'm calling you out. You heard me. I think you didn't show up because you're afraid to tell your story. Maybe you don't have a story?" Her face looked ugly in that moment.

"I'll be back on Facebook Live tonight, waiting for you. If you don't come, I'll know you're scared. Oh," she added like it just occurred to her. "I have a picture of you now. I'd hate to share that all over social media before you have a chance to tell your side." She finished her not-so-subtle threat and smiled. I was flabbergasted that she told the world we had the murderer's image.

"And, of course, for those of you watching, please share this all over social media, just in case the Firecracker Killer simply didn't know about my invitation last time. We'll be right back."

The show cut to commercial and I waited for it. My phone started dinging as texts poured in from Catherine and Jacob. As if I had any idea she would throw down the gauntlet like this. I'd give the woman credit, she was tenacious!

*****

It was Capture the Murderer, take two, that night at Liz's home. Light from streetlamps glinted off of what I imagined were camera lenses in a couple of cars. That was about it. The circus mostly stayed away tonight; I guess they decided it wasn't worth the time. Jacob came again, but he wasn't here in an official capacity and he had no additional officers. Metro was chronically understaffed and his supervisors didn't believe Liz's "publicity stunt" warranted allocation of officers again.

Catherine and Evie were also present, mainly because, like me, they were worried that Liz might have truly pissed the djinn off.

Due to the lack of official support, no homes had been commandeered and the three of them camped out in an SUV across the street. They planned to watch the Facebook Live streaming on Jacob's laptop.

I, however, was back in the office with Liz. She sat at her desk, gnawing on her lower lip. Worried about a repeat no-show performance? Or worried that the murderer *would* show up?

"Do you think she'll show up tonight?"

"I don't know," I answered. "She clearly didn't take the bait the first night, but the way you goaded her—"

Liz hung her head. "Yeah. I hope that wasn't a mistake."

"Do you actually want her to show up or not?"

"Yes," she answered, that hungry look back in her eyes. "Are you ever going to tell me how you figured out the murderer is Juni's sister?"

The question was asked offhand but I heard the real question. "Probably not," I admitted. "What makes you ask about it now?"

"I think there's stuff you're not telling me."

"Everybody has secrets."

"Indeed."

We stared at each other, both trying to read what the other was hiding. Did she know something? I walked back through our conversations; I didn't believe I'd let anything slip.

You guys ready? Five minutes until go time.

"You ready?" I asked Liz. "That was Jacob checking in."

"As ready as I'll ever be," she answered. I gave her a thumbs-up and walked back to the guest room where I stayed last time.

Liz's image glowed from my cellphone screen. I was seated in a bean bag chair, legs akimbo, the light from the screen all that was on in this part of her home. Again, I kept the sound off, but could hear her voice from the other room as the Liz on screen moved her lips.

"Welcome back to everyone who chose to join me again tonight."

There were some comments but it was definitely not flying fast and furious like before. I guessed much of the audience also stayed away.

"A few people have questioned whether it was smart of me to challenge a murderer the way that I did." I winced in the dark. Liz smiled.

"Probably not. But, when you want to get the story." She shrugged with this admission. The comments below were a mixture of admiration for her gutsy move and chiding her for being an idiot. I was undecided at this juncture. I still believed what I told the ladies the other night. Our best bet was to bring Juni's sister to us.

Liz continued to talk but I was no longer listening. Something changed. The air felt heavier. I'd actually never met a djinn before. I didn't know if this meant her essence had arrived. Liz still chatted as though nothing had changed. I wondered if it was my overactive imagination.

POP POP POP POP POP

Guess not. I bolted from the chair at the firecracker sounds, a hair after I noticed Liz's smile slip. The murderer was in the house.

"Hello? Is that you? Firecracker Killer?" Liz's voice wavered only a bit when she called out.

I crept to the edge of the bedroom door, peeked around the corner. The house remained dark. Popping sounds filled the air.

"Hello? For those watching from home, you can hear the familiar sounds that have preceded the Firecracker Killer's entrance on the prior three videos," Liz continued in her newscaster voice.

I entered the hallway and made my way toward the front office.

"I hear the popping but I still have no visual on who exactly is present," Liz told her audience. "Hello? Please identify yourself," Liz instructed the apparent presence.

I almost laughed but didn't want to give away my location.

No verbal response but, if anything, the popping sounded louder. It felt like a jackhammer in my skull. Something must be about to happen. I reached the final corner before the office. I rounded the corner, saw the office entrance five feet before me.

The air at the office door shimmered.

"Something is happening!" Liz told her audience.

I took a few tentative steps forward.

"A shape is forming in the doorway," Liz reported.

An outline of a figure appeared.

"There's someone—" She stopped speaking.

A feminine form had fully materialized.

CHAPTER NINETEEN

"There's a woman. She has long brown hair, black eyes." She stuttered on this descriptor. "Tan, maybe bronze skin." She paused as the popping stopped. Silence filled the house.

"Are you Juni's sister?" I broke the silence and the woman turned. I recoiled from the anger on her face.

"Mia, what are you doing?"

"Who are you?"

The woman did not speak but *Jena* floated in my mind. I stepped closer, could see into the office now.

"Jena?" I asked.

"Jena? Who's Jena? Is she Jena? What are you doing, Mia?" Liz spun her laptop in our direction and stepped around the far side of the desk, intent on regaining control of her interview. I only had a few minutes.

The woman, Jena, took a single step toward me.

"You don't have to do this," I told her. I lowered my voice. "We're like you; let us help you." Jena's face remained impassive. Liz's did not.

"What are you saying? Mia, what's going on?" Liz stepped within touching distance of Jena and a blinding light engulfed the room.

I waited for my eyes to readjust when the light vanished. Jena was gone. Liz lay on the floor. I moved toward her as the front door opened.

"Mia?! Liz?" I heard Jacob's voice and then hurried footsteps. I was cradling Liz's head in my lap when Jacob, Catherine, and Evie rushed into the room.

Relief flashed across their faces, presumably that I was okay, and then worry replaced it as they saw Liz.

"She's unconscious," I explained.

Jacob pulled his cellphone from his pocket to call for an ambulance. Catherine and Evie hung back.

"What happened?" Jacob resumed the detective role, and I gave a modified version of events. He quirked an eyebrow when I stated that I came around the corner and saw a woman standing in the doorway of the office.

"You didn't see or hear anything prior to that?"

"Just the popping noises."

"She just appeared?" Disbelief dripped from his words.

"I can only tell you I came around the corner and she was there," I insisted, which was a version of the truth.

"Stay here," he ordered and left to check all the windows and doors of the house.

Evie and Catherine moved in closer.

"What really happened?" Evie whispered.

I shook my head. "Wait until we're alone."

Flashing red and blue lights penetrated the window blinds. A few seconds later, emergency responders entered the home, followed closely by backup law enforcement. The EMS folks checked Liz's vitals – strong, it appeared – and lifted her onto a stretcher to carry to the ambulance. Catherine, Evie, and I watched in silence as they headed toward the door.

"Do any of you wish to accompany her?"

Catherine looked at me and Evie before answering the EMS woman in the affirmative.

"Thanks." I gave her a quick hug and she left with the ambulance. Evie and I remained in the office, leaning back against the desk, waiting. I imagined Jacob was not done with me yet.

Sure enough, after speaking with the backup officers briefly, he asked us to follow him outside. The officers were securing the scene. It was not clear a crime had been committed, or if the reported woman was the killer, but they weren't taking any chances.

Jacob indicated I should sit in the passenger seat of the SUV, while he got behind the wheel and Evie clambered into the backseat.

"What did you see during the streaming?" I asked.

Jacob gave me an inscrutable look then opened his laptop. "I recorded the video. This is what we saw." He pressed play. I watched the familiar opening, as Liz chattered. Popping sounds. Liz asking the murderer to show herself. Her look of surprise followed by a description of the woman. Then a muffled voice in the background. I was thankful you couldn't distinctly hear what I said. Liz questioning me, standing, spinning the laptop. I sighed in relief when the laptop stopped halfway around and faced the window. Jacob glanced at me sharply. Liz asked her final question, "Mia, what's going on?", the bright light flashed and the video stopped. It all happened much faster than I had thought.

"Mia, what *was* going on?"

I stared at Jacob, considering my response. "I've already told you what I saw."

"Why did Liz ask you that?"

I faltered this time. "I don't know." Weak. I knew it and Jacob knew it.

"Who is Jena?" Jacob stared at me through narrowed eyes.

I tried to think of a good explanation.

"It's not a trick question," he said drily.

"She's Juni's sister," I finally answered.

"The one you mentioned before," he confirmed.

"Yes."

"Are you ready yet to tell me how you found out about her?"

I swallowed audibly around the lump in my throat. "No."

"What else aren't you telling me?"

"I can't tell you anything else."

"Can't? Or won't?"

I remained silent.

A knock on the window broke the uncomfortable silence. Jacob started the car and rolled the window down.

"Sir. We were able to restart her computer." The officer handed Liz's laptop through the window. Jacob thanked him and rolled the window back up. The laptop actually appeared slightly singed; it was a miracle they were able to restart it.

Jacob opened the laptop, woke it from sleep mode, and clicked on Documents. His eyes scanned the rows and columns of icons. I couldn't see the details from here. Was he looking for something specific? He clicked on an icon and instead of a document, a video opened. Liz staring at the screen. Jacob hit play.

"Hello, this is Elizabeth Addison, coming to you from Las Vegas. As many of you know, I have been hot on the trail of the Firecracker Killer. This unknown person, recently identified as a woman, is possibly the sister of a woman murdered by the Firecracker Killer's first victim." Liz paused in the video and Jacob's eyes burned on me.

"If that sounds confusing, just wait. Today this case took on dimensions I never imagined." My mind raced to figure out what she was about to say. Liz's eyes practically glowed from her excitement, so I knew it must be big. On screen, Liz gulped a big breath. "I recently learned that there are supernatural beings living in Las Vegas."

My sharp intake of breath matched Evie's as Jacob muttered, "What the—"

Liz continued. "I have reason to believe that the murderer is not actually a woman after all, but a djinn, otherwise known as a genie. This previously believed-to-be mythical being—" Liz continued to talk but her voice had been replaced by a high-pitched whine in my ears.

How did she find out? And then I remembered my conversation with Catherine and Evie on the doorstep to Liz's house. Could she have overheard us somehow? I tilted my head back as a vague recollection of a security camera at her door floated to the surface of my memory. Did it have audio? Could she have turned it on to eavesdrop on us?

I tuned back in to Liz talking to the camera. "I also have reason to believe there is at least one supernatural being in the Valley capable of bewitching. This woman – whatever she is – can bend you to her will. And there's nothing you can do about it." On screen, Liz gave a final smile. "That's all I have for now, but I'll be back when I have more to report."

"Did she post this anywhere?"

"That's your reaction to the video?"

"What reaction did you want to see?" I asked softly.

"Maybe one more of surprise," he answered. "Like those of us who don't already know about the existence of these beings."

"You believe her crazy ramblings?" I asked with an arch of an eyebrow.

He didn't buy my nonchalance. "I heard your reaction when she said the killer is a genie. Don't insult me by trying to pretend otherwise." Hurt shined in his eyes as he looked at me; I dropped my gaze to my lap.

"I don't know what to say," I admitted.

"Evie, can you give us a minute?"

Without a word, Evie scrambled from the car.

"What did you say to the genie? To Jena?"

"I don't remember."

"You're lying. Are you involved with her?"

"What?!"

"Are you working with her?"

"No, of course not."

"You say that as though I can trust you." His voice was low with controlled anger. "If not for the supernatural stuff, I'd bring you in as a person of interest."

I closed my eyes against tears threatening to spill. "You'd arrest me?"

His voice softened. "I don't want to. But, you're not giving me anything. Help me out here," he begged.

Our eyes met. I reached out a hand to touch his cheek. The familiar snap of static electricity sounded and his cheek was rough against my fingers. We smiled before his slipped and his expression hardened. He jerked away from me.

"Are you the being Liz mentioned? Have you bewitched me? Does that explain this?" He gestured back and forth between us.

"No! Of course not!"

"No, you're not the being? Or, no, you haven't bewitched me? Can you bewitch people?"

I didn't answer.

"What are you?"

"I'm Mia."

"That's not an answer."

"That's the only answer I can give you."

CHAPTER TWENTY

Thank goodness it was midnight. I drove home from Liz's house in tears following my conversation with Jacob.

How could he possibly think I was working with a killer and I bewitched him?

Now I floated in the lake, recharging my energy. Tonight was way more emotional than I had anticipated. My fingers glided through the water, rubbed against curious fish, and my tension started to drain away.

Despite my efforts to keep my mind empty, thoughts of my failure returned. I wanted to understand why Jena was doing this. I wanted to reason with her to stop the killing. She seemed to be listening to me, until Liz interrupted. I sighed underwater, then laughed that there was still air in my lungs to push out.

What did I do now?

My thoughts turned to Liz. I had known she was up to something; I could tell by the sly glances and her reticence when she normally would bulldoze. It never occurred to me that she would have figured out about the paranormal. My role in her discovery saddened me. The paranormal underworld wanted to keep it that way. I hoped I hadn't put her at risk by exposing us – if she *outed* us. I couldn't imagine the fallout. The vampires in particular didn't take kindly to humans threatening their existence and they wouldn't hesitate to kill her.

I needed to talk to Evie. Actually, all of us needed to talk to Liz. Me, Evie, and Catherine. We had to explain the danger Liz could put herself in.

Hoisting myself out of the lake, I made my way into my home. Before I hopped in the shower, I texted the ladies. First Evie, who I knew was up; hopefully she was free.

Are you available? Meet me at the hospital. We need to talk to Liz.

And then Catherine, who might still be at the hospital. She hadn't texted an update.

You still at the hospital? Evie and I are coming. We need to talk to Liz.

Their affirmative responses arrived as I lathered. I texted them again before I backed out of the garage; I estimated fifteen minutes to the hospital and said I'd meet them in the lobby.

"How is she doing?" I greeted Catherine with the question and a hug.

"She's sleeping. I overheard the doctor telling Jacob that she's not in a coma and could wake up anytime."

"Jacob was here? How did he seem?"

"Seem?"

Oh right, Catherine wasn't there for any of our disagreement. "When Evie gets here, I'll bring you up to speed."

"I'm here," came a voice behind me. Catherine and I hugged Evie.

I summarized my conversation with Jacob. They stared at me in silence. "Relax, nobody died." I tried for light-hearted and failed.

"What do we want to say to Liz?" Evie asked this, changing the subject, for which I was grateful.

"Follow my lead?"

Catherine and Evie agreed to do so and Catherine led the way to Liz's room. Since she was mainly here for observation, she was in a regular, though private, room, and not the ER or ICU. Beeping machinery greeted us. Liz didn't look bad; she really did look like she was just sleeping, if not for the few wires monitoring her status.

"Should we wake her?"

"No need, Evie," answered the woman in question. She opened her eyes and smiled weakly at us. "I'm awake. Thanks for staying with me Catherine."

"I didn't know you knew I was here."

"I did."

A moment passed. Liz knew we were not there just to check on her, but she'd clearly decided to let us direct the conversation.

"Jacob is going to want to talk to you," I started. She nodded. "He thinks I'm working with Jena." Her eyes widened at that. "I was hoping that when you speak with him, you can straighten that misperception out."

"How do I know you aren't working with Jena?"

I gaped at her. "I've been working with you the whole time!"

"You've kept secrets from me the whole time." One hospital gown clad shoulder lifted. "How do I know you weren't hiding that too?"

I turned to Catherine and Evie for help. They looked stunned. Catherine was the first to jump in to defend me. "Liz, you haven't known Mia that long, but I can personally assure you that she's not a killer. In any way, shape, or form," she emphasized.

Liz's lip curled. "That and a couple of bucks will get me a cup of coffee."

"How could you think she's a killer?" Evie asked. "Aren't you a better journalist than that to be taken in?"

Risky to insult the woman whose cooperation we wanted, but when Liz's cheeks reddened I realized Evie took the right approach.

Liz sighed. "I know she's not involved," she allowed. "I'm just pissed you guys didn't tell me about the paranormal world."

"You'll tell Jacob I wasn't involved?"

"Yes, Mia, I'll tell Jacob you weren't involved." She paused. "If you do something for me."

"You're going to extort Mia? For you to tell the truth?" Evie sounded pissed. I didn't blame her; I wasn't feeling too charitable.

I headed off the ensuing battle. "What do you want?"

"Information."

We didn't have to ask what kind of information; we all knew what she wanted to know. "I can't give you what you want," I said.

"Then I can't say what you want." She pointedly closed her eyes. "You can go."

"We're doing this to protect you," Catherine insisted.

Liz opened a single eye. "Go on."

"We can confirm the paranormal underworld exists, but most of us want to keep it that way," Evie explained.

"And?"

"If you threaten to out us, you'll be killed," Evie responded simply.

"Us?"

I was really hoping that Liz would have missed that pronoun, so of course she didn't.

"I'm a vampire."

Liz stared open-mouthed at Evie. "A what?"

"You heard me. And my people will kill you without hesitation if you try to tell the world about us."

"You're a vampire?" Liz repeated.

"Yes. Keep up," Evie snapped.

"Okay."

"That's it? Okay?"

"What more do you want, Mia? I'll inform Jacob that you were not involved in any of the murders. I will also not disclose the existence of a paranormal underworld."

I breathed a sigh of relief.

"For now," Liz continued.

"For now?" Catherine questioned.

"There's an echo in this room," Liz retorted.

"Don't be a bitch," Evie snapped.

"Evie!" Catherine exclaimed.

"Sorry," Evie said, not sounding sorry.

"What do you mean, for now?" I redirected.

"Well, Mia, I want the whole story. I want Jena and the paranormal underworld." She smiled shrewdly. "If I wait for Jena to be caught, then I can have both. So, I'll wait," she concluded.

The three of us goggled at her.

"What about the risk to your life?" I had to think that self-preservation would be high on Liz's list of importance.

"Once I actually out all of you," she said, and I sensed that Evie wanted to knock the smug look off of Liz's face, "nobody would dare kill me."

Evie snorted. "Like my people care. You'll just have an 'accident'," she explained, putting the last word in air quotes.

"I'll take that chance."

This was probably the best we were going to do tonight. At least Liz wasn't going to say anything more about us right now and she'd clear things up with Jacob. We'd have to be satisfied with that.

"Thank you," was all I said.

Liz gestured for us to leave. "I'm tired. We'll talk later."

"Actually, Liz, now that I know your full plan, I don't think it's in anybody's best interest for us to continue to work together on this story."

"So be it, Mia," she answered and closed her eyes.

We took that as our unsubtle cue to leave and did. We remained silent walking down the hallway away from her room. I noticed an empty darkened room to our left and ducked inside. Catherine and Evie followed.

"What do you guys think?" I asked.

"We probably should report her." Evie said this but I could tell her heart wasn't in it.

"If we do, she'll be dead within twenty-four hours." Vampires had Cleaners for exactly this sort of job.

"I know."

We considered our options. We were all uncomfortable with the idea of signing Liz's death warrant.

"What happens if you don't?" Catherine asked.

"If the Family finds out after the fact, and they believe we knew, we're probably dead for not saying anything."

I expected this answer but Catherine clearly didn't. "You're kidding."

Evie and I shook our heads no.

"Well, dang, what do we do?" Catherine asked.

"If I may give an opinion?"

We turned as one to face the woman who had entered the room.

"Robin?" Catherine asked in distaste.

"Hello, ladies," Robin Landon addressed us. "I couldn't help but overhear—"

"Because you were eavesdropping," Evie interrupted.

"—your quandary," Robin continued as though uninterrupted.

We stared at her for a beat.

"And you have an opinion?" I asked.

"I do. I wanted to let you know not to worry so much about this," she said easily.

"Really? What does the councilwoman have to do with this?"

"Tsk, tsk, Mia," Robin scolded. "You know I won't answer that question. The councilwoman simply wanted you to know that she would take care of it."

"Take care of it," Catherine gulped. "Is she going to kill Liz?"

Robin laughed. "Not at the present time." We stared at her when she didn't continue. She sighed. "You're still on the right path. Liz is playing her part."

And with that, the demon's minion exited the room. We stood in silence for a moment.

"Okay, what do you guys think?" Catherine finally asked.

"Not to give Robin or Barbara too much credit, but my vote is we don't say anything. The Councilwoman told me before that I was on the right track. And now Robin says not to worry about it. Regardless of their involvement, I won't be able to sleep knowing I had a hand in someone's death," I finished and the other two nodded.

"Besides," I added with a hopeful smile, "maybe Liz is right. Maybe they won't kill her if she goes public, since she is a celebrity of sorts, and not just a random fruit loop on the internet."

"That is optimistic," Evie said, sounding doubtful.

"Yeah, I know, but what else have we got?"

"Maybe Barbara really will keep her safe?" Catherine asked.

"If that's actually what Robin meant," I countered.

"Maybe we can talk Liz out of it," Catherine offered.

"Unlikely, but there's no harm in trying," I agreed.

CHAPTER TWENTY-ONE

Back home, I was debating whether or not to slip into the lake or the pool when my house and mind filled with all-too-familiar popping sounds. I froze in my living room, head swinging side to side to see where Jena would materialize.

Next to my glass topped wicker breakfast table, I saw the shimmer in the air that preceded Jena's arrival before. I braced myself, wondering inanely whether or not she was coming in peace. Like she was an alien or something.

Jena appeared before me, her black eyes flashing like obsidian glowing from within. She glared; I remained silent. Waiting.

"How did you find me?"

No small talk for the genie I gathered. "You were captured on a vacationer's video; from there we found you on security footage at a casino."

"Who are you?"

"My name is Mia. I'm a movie producer. You killed," I swallowed audibly, "one of my actors. Chad Johnson." No reaction. "I'm also a nixie."

"Why did you want to find me?"

Her monotone voice unsettled me. "I wanted to help you."

"Help me how?"

"You can stop doing this."

"Why would I stop?"

Unsure what to say, I shifted. "How did you start?"

She stared as if trying to determine whether or not to tell me. If she wanted to kill me, she probably could before I could react.

"A year ago, my sister Juni Jawahir was killed by the human, Roger Miller."

"It was an accident."

She glared at me for the interruption. "I waited for the human system to bring him to justice, but they let him go." Her body hummed with hatred.

"I knew I had to have patience. I waited for a sufficient amount of time to pass. Even though I wanted revenge, I did not want to unduly bring attention to our kind," she anticipated my question.

"After a year, I decided enough time had passed and I exacted my revenge." She stopped like that was the end of the story.

"What about Chad? And Bradley Reese?"

"People like Roger care only for themselves. They care only about what other people can do for them. The fewer of them that exist in the world, the better the world will be."

"That's why you targeted actors? Because you think they care only for themselves?"

"Yes."

I was silent and she continued. "Once I killed Roger, I searched online for an actor promoting an upcoming Facebook Live streaming video. After I found Chad, I searched for him in person, followed him off and on. I decided he was the one. I waited for my moment."

Nausea bubbled up and Jena must have seen something in my face.

"Roger, Chad, Bradley. They're all the same. They wanted internet fame. I gave it to them."

Her complete lack of remorse unnerved me, but I pressed forward. "Not all actors are like that. Chad was a young man doing what he loved. Wanting to share that with the world."

A flicker of uncertainty crossed her face. "No."

"Yes, Jena. Even Roger's involvement with Juni's death was a horrible, horrible accident. He was devastated by her loss. He loved her. Surely you saw his social media posts when you were—" I paused to find another word for *stalking* "—gathering information."

Jena didn't respond.

"Jena, you can stop. Your existence can go back to normal."

"I don't want to."

Stunned by her admission, I struggled to find anything else to say. My secret goal, once I knew that the killer was a supernatural being, was to find out why and possibly help him or her without resorting to killing the being. And once I knew she was a djinn, I immediately recognized either she stopped or she was killed. I still didn't see another possible outcome. She was too powerful. I had to convince her to stop killing men.

"Why?"

"Because it's fun. These men don't deserve the life they've been given. I'm solving that."

"I can't let you keep—"

Jena laughed, an unearthly sound. "Let? As if you could do anything to stop me."

"I'm going to try."

"Don't make me kill you too." She dematerialized.

I collapsed on the couch, my heart racing. I failed. Other men were going to die unless I found a way to kill her. Dawn was a few hours away. I curled up on the couch for some relaxation before making another move.

The next morning, my heart in my throat, I called Jacob. It went to voicemail and I wondered if he was there and choosing not to answer.

"Hey, Jacob," I started, after the beep. "If you have some time, I'd really like to talk to you. It's important. It'll answer a bunch of your questions."

I ended the call. I didn't say I'd answer *all* of his questions, but maybe it was time to tell him at least a little bit more. If Jena wasn't going to stop, then anybody chasing after her was in danger.

My phone trilled notification of an incoming call. Jacob.

"Hey, Jacob."

"Hi, Mia."

Silence.

"You left me a voicemail."

"I did. Um." I paused.

"Mia, I don't have time for this."

The coldness in his voice hurt. "Can we meet?"

"I'd rather you tell me over the phone."

My eyes filled with tears. "I'd rather tell you in person."

"Fine. Text me where and when and I'll be there." He ended the call.

I held the silent phone in my hand, in shock. He hung up on me. I decided my place gave us the privacy I wanted given the subject matter. Hands shaking, I texted him my address to meet in one hour. I didn't know where he was in the city right now and I didn't want to be difficult.

Wait a minute. He was the one freezing me out. He wanted to keep it professional, I could keep it professional. A wave of sadness crashed over me at the thought of not touching him again or seeing his smile.

Whatever. He made his choice.

CHAPTER TWENTY-TWO

Exactly an hour later, my doorbell chimed. I opened the door and our eyes met. His were hard marbles in a granite face. He followed me to my breakfast nook.

"Please sit," I said and gestured to the wicker chair opposite me.

We sat simultaneously. He removed a small notebook and pen from his sports jacket inner pocket. "What do you have for me?"

"Jena appeared in my home," I started without preamble and that got his attention. I saw the worry in his eyes for a moment before the shutter dropped again.

"Appeared?"

"Yes." I explained to Jacob exactly what a djinn was and Jena's connection to Juni, as well as her admitting to me that she was the killer. "I am not working with her," I added.

"I know. Ms. Addison confirmed that when I spoke with her this morning."

My breath whooshed out in relief. "Okay, good."

"Is that it?"

"No. You may be in danger." I explained Jena's threat to harm anyone who got in her way.

"Can she be stopped?"

That was the million-dollar question, right? "Probably not," I admitted. "Not without killing her."

"How do we kill her?"

"Just how Juni died; her heart has to be pierced."

"How do we get to her?"

I chuckled. "You don't."

"That's not helpful."

My voice rose. "Well, forgive me for not wanting to be so quick to kill her."

"She's a murderer. And you just said the only way to stop her is to kill her, Mia!" His voice had risen to match mine.

"She's hurt because Roger killed her sister," I tried to remind him. "She's acting out of a weird warped grief."

"Are you seriously making excuses for the monster serial killer?"

I recoiled as if slapped. "Monster?"

Guilt clouded his face. "That isn't what I meant."

"Sure, it is."

"Mia—"

"You see me as a monster," I whispered.

"I don't know what to see you as," he argued. "You won't tell me who you are!" He stood and strode from the table toward the kitchen. He gripped the countertop with both hands. I stood and took a few steps toward him but stopped.

"Why does it matter so much what category I am?"

He faced me, anguish warring with anger on his face. "Because I don't understand. Any of this." He raked his hand through his hair. "What if you become like her?"

"Now I'm not just a monster, but you think I could be a killer?!"

"You tried to justify her actions and you don't want her to be harmed!"

We were yelling at each other when we both heard a popping noise. I scanned the room and, over the kitchen passthrough, I saw the shimmer in the living room. Jacob drew his gun as Jena completed her materializing.

"Jacob, no!" I shouted, but I was too late.

The shot rang out. Jena jerked backward against the couch. The anger in her eyes scared me. The popping increased exponentially in volume. Jacob covered one ear while training his gun on her figure by the couch. A second shot rang out. She reappeared between me and Jacob.

"I won't let you hurt her," Jena told Jacob. She stepped toward him, arms outstretched.

"Jena, no! He's not trying to hurt me!"

Jacob raised his gun again. Jena had reached him, grabbed him around the throat. His face mottled as he failed to draw in air.

"Jena, no!" I screamed again. I took several steps toward her. She whipped her face around to glare daggers at me.

"It's better this way. He'll only hurt you in the end."

She turned back to face Jacob, whose eyes now showed only the whites. He stopped struggling.

Unthinking, I grabbed a large knife from the wooden block on the counter. Jena's head turned toward me when the tip of the knife entered flesh.

The hurt I saw in her eyes wounded me. She tried to dematerialize but it was too late. Her eyes widened a final time before she turned to water and drenched me and Jacob, who had slumped to the floor.

I killed her.

To save him.

The conflicting statements spun around in my mind.

I wanted to go to him, but instead I sat at the table, lay my head on the top. Tears fell while I waited for him to regain consciousness. As he did, he leapt to his feet, surprised by his unsteadiness, gun in his outstretched arm. He spun, looking for Jena. Did not react when all he saw was me.

"Where is she? Where is Jena?"

I lifted my head, the tears still falling. "She's gone, Jacob."

"Gone? Where did she go?"

"Dead," I whispered.

That got his attention. He lowered his gun, really saw me. "Dead?"

My watery eyes met his. "I killed her."

"To save me."

I jolted at the words in my mind spoken aloud. "Yes."

He sat across from me again. "You did the right thing."

"Did I?"

"Yes, she was going to kill more people. You said so yourself."

"She was only trying to protect me."

"What?"

"Just now. She thought you were going to hurt me. She was confused. She was only trying to protect me." The tears fell faster and hotter now. I had never killed anyone before, let alone a fellow paranormal being. It felt horrible.

Jacob appeared shocked. "I would never hurt you."

I gave him a crooked smile. "I know that. She didn't. She thought she was protecting me," I repeated.

Jacob reached for me and I jerked backwards, up and out of the seat.

The pain consumed me and I needed to be away from this. From him. From where I killed her. I shook my head to knock the thoughts loose, but it didn't work.

"I have to go," I told Jacob. A strange white noise filled my mind. A low hum that was probably Jacob's voice tried to filter through but was unable.

"I have to go," I repeated, as I opened the sliding glass door. Even though it was the middle of a bright, sunny day, I needed my refuge. I needed my water. I needed to recharge.

I walked, fully clothed, down the stairs of my pool and settled at the bottom. That white noise continued with the low hum beneath. I ignored both and focused on the feeling of the water. A dark shadow appeared on the concrete of the other side of the pool.

I saw Jacob pacing, yelling at me in the water. I ignored him. He jumped into the water, grabbed me, and pulled me to the surface. He was spluttering as we broke through the water. I was weightless in his arms, not fighting or helping him. He brushed my hair off of my face.

"Mia, what are you doing?! This isn't the answer."

I stared into his face and then laughed morosely. "You think I'm trying to kill myself?"

He looked confused. "Aren't you?"

"No."

"Then why weren't you resurfacing?"

I was acutely aware of his arms around me now and the heat suffused my body. "I don't need to resurface," I explained without thinking. I cuddled in closer. He tensed but held me. Then the guilt returned. I killed someone. I struggled against him and he released me.

We stood before each other in my pool. His eyes a torrent of confusion, desire, and fear.

"You should go," I told him before sinking back to the bottom of the pool. He remained standing there for several long minutes, watching me, waiting to see what happened. I closed my eyes to leave him to it. I guessed he must have seen whatever it was he needed, because underwater waves jostled me as he exited the pool.

CHAPTER TWENTY-THREE

The next morning probably dawned sunny and warm, but I didn't know, because I never left my bed. Shades drawn kept my bedroom in relative darkness, tiny slivers of light peeking around the edges of the wood blinds.

My phone remained on silent. I imagined people were trying to reach me, but I didn't care. My thoughts were a maelstrom. This was what it had come to.

I killed someone. A paranormal being driven mad by grief, true. But still. With more time, maybe I could have helped her. I killed her to protect a man who thought I was a freak. At least nobody else would die. This was cold comfort as I curled into a ball under my comforter.

Other than a banana and bathroom breaks, I stayed in bed watching the sun through the blinds march across the sky and become dusk. I started to feel weirdly self-indulgent spending the day in bed. I sat up and stretched, grabbed my phone off the nightstand. Dang, my phone blew up while I was sleeping. Notifications of texts, phone calls, and voicemails filled the screen. Catherine and Evie, of course. Jacob. That one surprised me. He made his feelings pretty clear before he left yesterday. Well, before I fled and hid from him under the water, I supposed was the more accurate description. I sighed and began checking each of the texts and calls.

My doorbell chimed as I reached the final of the increasingly frantic messages from my friends. I had a feeling I knew who was there, once I confirmed with a glance at the blinds that night had fallen. I also had a feeling I knew who wasn't at the door. Jacob called twice but didn't leave a message either time. I left the warm comfort of the bed and threw on a satin robe before heading downstairs.

The doorbell chimed a second time. I opened the door. "You ladies are impatient."

Catherine and Evie threw themselves at me in a group hug.

"We were so worried!"

"I gave you until Evie woke up, but when you didn't respond, we decided an intervention was in order."

"You can't ignore us," Evie added. "We're your friends."

Catherine held up a bottle of wine. "We brought liquid libations."

Evie held up a gallon of chocolate chip cookie dough ice cream. "And comfort food."

I smiled at their enthusiasm. "Not that you can have either."

Evie pointed to her bag. "Not to worry. I brought a bottle of my sustenance too."

The three of us laughed as the women entered my home behind me. We paused in the kitchen to pour the drinks and scoop the ice cream. Then we collapsed on the couch.

Concerned eyes stared at me. I broke eye contact and stared instead at my fidgeting fingers.

"What happened, Mia? Jacob called me several times, asking about you. He said Jena was gone."

My eyes filled with tears. I looked at Catherine. "He called you?"

"He did. He wouldn't tell me anything else."

"What happened?" Evie echoed Catherine.

I inhaled a deep breath and told the whole ugly story of my fight with Jacob, Jena's misguided intervention, and my killing her. Both women gasped when I got to that part and my tears flowed freely.

"Oh, Mia. I'm so sorry you had to go through that," Catherine said softly. She leaned in to give me a tight hug. I took strength from her embrace, smelled the subtle scent of lavender.

"Thank you."

"You know there was nothing else you could have done, right?" Evie asked this pointedly. I shook my head. "Seriously, Mia, misguided or not, Jena was a serial killer. She was unstable. You saved lives by taking hers."

"That sounds all well and good," I responded more sharply than I intended. "But the bottom line is that I killed her when she was trying to help me." I gasped for air when the tears came harder.

Evie rose. She paced back and forth in front of us. "Bullshit," she finally said and my mouth fell open.

"What—"

"Don't give me that bullshit. I know what it's like to take a life, remember." I saw the haunted look in her eyes, a reflection of her own experience only a few months ago.

"Sometimes it's necessary. Killing Jena was inevitable. I can't believe you thought you'd be able to talk her down." She shook her head.

Her words both hurt and comforted me. "I'll never know," I argued and she cut me off with a flick of her wrist.

"Yes. You do. You're hurting because you know this was always going to be the outcome and you were deluding yourself thinking otherwise. You agree, right, Catherine?"

We both looked at Catherine, who held her hands up in the universal sign of *don't drag me into the middle of this.*

"You both have legitimate points." We waited for her to continue but she didn't. "That's all." She smiled serenely.

And for some reason, that turned the tide for me. I laughed, a deep belly laugh that might have cracked a rib if I kept going too long. It felt good, though, that laugh.

Catherine and Evie looked at me askance for a moment, looked at each other with a smile, and then all three of us were on the couch, laughing and hugging each other. I accepted this release and comfort.

I wiped tears from my eyes, of laughter not pain this time. "Wiser words were never spoken, Catherine." I held each of their hands.

"Thank you both for coming here. You are absolutely right. I probably was delusional to think I could talk an irrational immortal being out of destruction. At least it's over now and nobody else will be hurt. I can't lay around feeling sorry for myself. What would that accomplish?"

"Exactly," Evie concurred.

"Thanks, Evie, for being so blunt. And thanks, Catherine, for being so … accommodating." I smiled and then my mouth turned down.

"What?" Catherine squeezed my hand.

"Jacob?" Evie asked. I nodded.

"Yeah. I thought whatever spark," I chuckled at the memories of the actual sparks flying, "we had might have led to something. He thinks I'm a monster." My voice fell to a whisper on the last word.

"Maybe," Catherine said. "But, he called you—"

"Didn't leave messages," I interrupted.

"He called me. He asked how you were doing. I wouldn't be so quick to dismiss him. Remember when I found out about Alex?" Her hunky boyfriend, Alexander Moore, was a half-incubus. "I needed time to process." She shrugged. "My guess is that Jacob felt blindsided, like I did, and needed time."

"And Ryan?" Evie asked. Her human boyfriend hadn't exactly jumped with excitement when he learned she was a vampire.

Hope glowed within me. "Do you really think?"

Catherine and Evie nodded.

I steeled myself and released their hands. "I'm going to put everything out there." I felt their eyes on me. I texted Jacob one last time. It was longer than I usually text, and probably I should have just called, but this was easier, and I still felt raw from his rejection. I hit send after typing the final line and smiled at my friends.

The ball is in your court now, as they say.

CHAPTER TWENTY-FOUR

I was impressed with myself that I did not continually check my phone for missed texts and calls from Jacob all night. I knew my phone was working. The lack of a text or a call by the next morning told me everything I needed to know. Maybe he called yesterday because he was simply a good guy. He wanted to make sure I was okay, but like a police officer checked in on a crime victim. Just doing his job. Not interested in more.

I swallowed past the lump in my throat and headed downstairs to make coffee. It was almost time for *Entertainment Daily*. I was curious if Jacob updated Liz like he said he would once the murders were solved.

"Good morning in the Valley! Welcome to *Entertainment Daily*. I'm your host, Elizabeth Addison." The smile dropped from her airbrushed-to-perfection face. Faux concern replaced it.

Stop it, I chided myself for my uncharitable thoughts. She was not a bad person, just career-driven.

"Many of you have been following the Firecracker Killer case for the past couple of weeks. I promised that I would inform all of you at the conclusion of the case. Well, that time has come. Citizens of the Valley, as well as Los Angeles, can breathe a sigh of relief that the Firecracker Killer is no more. But, let me warn you, this next part may sound outrageous, like a pathetic attempt to boost ratings. Most of you will want to dismiss what I say as pure nonsense. I understand. I felt the same way when I first heard about it." She paused dramatically and my heart was in my throat because I knew what she was about to say.

"How many of you have watched television and movies about vampires and genies? How many of you have laughed instead of been afraid because you knew it was fake?"

I put my hands over my mouth. She wasn't going to out us. She couldn't out us. Then I reminded myself that she said this was her goal. I closed my eyes for a moment, breathed deeply.

"I am here to tell you that it's real. I know, I know. It can't possibly be true. Let me tell you a story. You may remember when I exclusively reported I was in possession of a photo of the Firecracker Killer. Many of you tuned in to my Facebook Live where the killer failed to show; not very many of you tuned in for the second attempt. You missed a doozy if that's the case." An image of Jena appeared in the corner of the screen. Liz gestured to it. "This individual, Jena Jawahir, appeared. And I mean appeared. She shimmered into being in front of me, those popping sounds we all recognize now, preceding her. I tried to talk to her; I learned her name. And then she vanished just like that." Liz snapped her fingers; I couldn't believe she was telling the world, but at least it seemed she wasn't going to mention me. Yet, anyway.

"She later appeared in a private home, where she admitted, in the presence of law enforcement, that she was the Firecracker Killer. She attacked said law enforcement representative and then a brave citizen, at great risk to herself, killed the killer in self-defense." Liz paused again. She clearly relished the telling of this story.

"You may be wondering about this creature who could appear and disappear at will. I have come to learn that she is what's known as a djinn, genie to most of us. But she doesn't grant wishes." Liz provided a brief definition and explanation about genies. It seemed mostly taken from Wikipedia but was fairly accurate.

"So, who was Jena Jawahir?" There followed a timeline of Juni's death in Roger's car accident, the justice system releasing him, and then Jena's three murders.

"This genie would not have stopped – she said as much – had she not been killed." This conclusion seemed directed at me. Did Jacob tell her that I'd been feeling guilty?

"Now the big question. Was she alone? I'm here to inform you that she was not. She was alone in the killing, yes, but there is an entire paranormal underworld existing in Las Vegas. In addition to the genie, we have vampires and beings who can bewitch you with their voices. And that's just scratching the surface." Thank goodness for small favors, I guess, that she had not identified my species yet. I refocused as she continued.

"You know I don't usually track rumors." I arched an eyebrow. Really? "But, I've also heard that there's a whole agency providing representation for actors of the other-than-human persuasion." How did she find out about Catherine?!

"It seems as though we have become ground zero for the paranormal. If you've had any unexplainable things happen to you, I want to know about them. The paranormal exist – we need to know how far their reach goes!" With that and a self-satisfied smirk, she signed off. I fumed that she would sensationalize our existence, imply that we were somehow a threat. Sure, we had more abilities than humans, but except for the vampire Cleaners, we mostly left humanity alone. Sheesh.

I clicked off the television. A text notification pinged. Hope bloomed. Jacob?

CHAPTER TWENTY-FIVE

My hope dashed when I saw the text was from Catherine.

How did she find out about PTA???

I thought for a moment of possible ways.

I don't know. Could Evie have told her after she admitted being a vampire?

Yeah, maybe. I don't think she would have unless she thought she was protecting us in some way.

That makes sense.

I'll check in with her tonight. Maybe ask her what the Family thinks.

Sounds good.

I supposed it really didn't matter how Liz found out. Once the paranormal cat was out of the bag, nothing was going to stop Liz from digging until she found the answers she wanted. I sighed, wondering if she'd reach out to me again or not. And what my reaction would be if she did. More importantly, I wondered if the Family would eliminate her. I suspected Liz was right, though; she was too visible to be taken out now without drawing undue suspicion.

A knock disturbed my thoughts. I was thankful for the interruption and headed to open the door.

"Jacob!"

"Hi, Mia." He searched my face, for what I was uncertain.

I gestured inward. "Did you want to come in?"

A smile lit up his face. "Yes."

I followed him, confused thoughts swirling in my mind. Why was he here? I appreciated the view of his backside as we walked to my couch. We sat, our knees inches apart. The air between us charged.

"What can I do for you, Jacob?"

"I saw Liz's show."

"Ah."

"I wanted to, um, check on you."

"You did?"

Hurt shined in his eyes at my question. "You don't think I'd be worried about you?"

I shrugged. "I honestly don't know. We didn't leave things very…positive."

His cheeks reddened. "I didn't know what to say before. I don't like being lied to."

"I don't think I lied to you. Lie of omission, maybe."

He reached for my hands, the familiar spark making us both smile. "That's not what I meant. I'm screwing this up." His hands tightened around mine. "I'm not blaming you for anything. I missed you."

"It's only been a day."

"I still missed you."

"Me too."

We sat in silence, lost in each other's eyes. Then he frowned. "But, this—" He released me and stood. He walked to my sliding glass doors, stared out at the water, or maybe the mountains in the distance.

"Is what we feel real? Liz said you can bewitch people with your voice." He turned and I saw the fear and desire.

"Yes," I responded simply. "That's true. I can entrance people."

"Entrance," he repeated with a nod.

I approached him. When he stiffened, I stopped, tears pooling in my eyes. "I didn't do that to you. I promise." Some of the tension bled away, but I still felt a wall between us.

"Let me tell you who I am and then you can decide if that's something you want—" I coughed "—can live with." He nodded. "Although I am humanoid, I'm not human. I am a nixie." I chuckled at his confusion. "Most people have never heard of us. A nix, or a naiad, is a water spirit." Understanding dawned in his eyes.

"When you stayed underwater without breathing?"

"Exactly. A nixie can live on the land, obviously, but needs to return to the water regularly to stay alive."

"You live in a desert," he contradicted with a smile.

"I do. Hide in plain sight, right? Besides, why do you think I live in The Lakes? And have a pool?"

"Makes sense." His eyes clouded again. "What about—?"

I blew out my breath, knowing this was the make or break moment for us. "Nixie are sometimes called sirens. Are you familiar with them? You could say we're cousins. They're the more destructive members of our family." He reflected my smile.

"Yes, I can entrance people with my voice. I'm quite the spellbinding singer, in fact. But," I frowned, "I don't like doing it and so only do it when I feel that it's truly necessary. I've never done it to someone I … cared … about."

"You care about me?" Desire pooled in his eyes.

I caressed his cheek, feeling the bristly stubble. He must not have shaved this morning. "I do."

His hand captured mine against his face and he brought my palm to his lips for a delicate kiss. "I care about you too."

Tingles shot through me at his words and his touch. I leaned forward in anticipation but he leaned back, releasing my hands. "What?"

He looked so earnest I almost laughed but my stomach rumbled with worry. "I need to apologize," he started.

"That's not—" I interrupted to tell him it wasn't necessary but stopped.

Jacob smiled crookedly. "Yeah, it's necessary," he responded to my unspoken sentiment. "You frustrated me." I opened my mouth to object. "Please, let me say this." I closed my mouth and nodded.

"You frustrated me," he repeated. "Because of my insane attraction to you." We both smiled. "And also, because I knew you were keeping something from me. I never thought you were a killer. But, I knew it was something. Being another species is a pretty big *something*."

He stared at me and I could feel the electricity in the air between us. I wanted more than anything in this moment for him to take me in his arms.

"Then I had to worry that what I felt wasn't real."

I couldn't help it, I interrupted. "I never entranced you. You just legitimately find me sexy."

Jacob laughed a deep belly laugh. "I know. I believe you. And, I definitely find you sexy."

"The feeling is mutual."

"I'm glad."

Unable to wait for him to make his move, I wrapped my arms around him and rested my head against his shoulder. I listened to his heart beat and his breathing. "Oh, and I'm about 200-years-old." His arms tightened around me for a moment and then relaxed. He chuckled, low and sexy.

"Man, you are really robbing the cradle, aren't you?"

The last of my tension dissipated and I pulled back to gaze into his eyes. "Yes, I am," I said with a smirk. "There's a lot about me that you still don't know."

"I look forward to learning every single thing," he assured me.

The heat and electricity between us increased. "Kiss me."

Jacob did. A sigh escaped me. His lips, sweetly at first and then with more insistence, pressed against mine. I didn't know where we were headed, in this moment or as a couple. Right now, this was all I cared about. Being together. After our long lingering kiss, Jacob pulled away and I saw the light in his eyes.

"By the way, what are you going to do about Liz's big reveal?"

"I don't know. We're all out of the closet now. I guess that's a wrap!"

Or is it?

Here's a sneak peek at Episode 4…

EPISODE FOUR PREVIEW

As the founder and owner of Landon Talent Agency, could I ever have predicted I'd make a deal with the devil? Okay, technically, Barbara Knollman was a low-level demon. But still. I'd agreed to do the demon's bidding and, if I wasn't entirely sorry for having made that deal, I definitely had regrets.

Now I sat in the overstuffed leather chair opposite the Councilwoman, my hands clasped in my lap, eyes downcast, like I'd been called to the principal's office. Though, in a way, that was true.

"Robin, this has worked out perfectly," Barbara intoned. She stood at the window overlooking Main Street, immobile, her brown hair swept back in a tight bun. She returned to her chair behind the imposing solid wood desk and sat, her hands resting on its surface, talon-like fingernails displayed.

The effect worked.

I swallowed audibly and Barbara chuckled.

"You really wanted the paranormal underworld to be exposed like this?" I asked.

Barbara smiled, her small sharp teeth drawing attention. "Yes. I did. I foresaw the path to my success. It included the exposure," she explained, tapping her manicured talons against the fine wood-grain.

"I'm not sure I understand what this has been about," I admitted in a small voice.

Barbara looked condescendingly down on me, her minion. "I know. You will. Everyone will."

Pick up Episode 4 from your favorite retailer today!

THANK YOU!

Thank you so much for supporting my work and reading this book. I truly hope you enjoyed reading it as much as I did writing it.

If you liked the book, please consider leaving a review online.

Just a few lines would be great. Reviews are not only the highest compliment you can pay to an author, they also help other readers discover and make more informed choices about purchasing books in a crowded online space. Thank you so much in advance.

If you didn't like the book or have concerns, please email me directly at
heather@heathersilvio.com

ABOUT THE AUTHOR

Heather has written fiction and nonfiction; she is also an actress and licensed psychologist. When she isn't working, she channels her inner flapper as a 1920s jazz and blues singer.

Visit http://www.heathersilvio.com for more information and to sign up for her New Releases and Appearances Newsletter.